BY SAMUEL R. DELANY

FICTION

The Jewels of Aptor (1962)
The Fall of the Towers
  Out of the Dead City (1963)
  The Towers of Toron (1964)
  City of a Thousand Suns (1965)
The Ballad of Beta-2 (1965)
Babel-17 (1966)
Empire Star (1966)
The Einstein Intersection (1967)
Nova (1968)
Driftglass (1969)
Equinox (1973)
Dhalgren (1975)
Trouble on Triton (1976)
Return to Neveryon
  Tales of Neveryon (1979)
  Neveryóna (1982)
  Flight from Neveryon (1985)
  Return to Neveryon (1987)
Distant Stars (1981)
Stars in My Pocket Like Grains of Sand (1984)
Driftglass/Starshards (collected stories, 1993)
They Fly at Ciron (1993)
The Mad Man (1994)
Hogg (1995)
Atlantis: Three Tales (1995)
Aye, and Gomorrah (and other stories, 2004)
Phallos (2004)
Dark Reflections (2007)
Through the Valley of the Nest of Spiders (2012)
A, B, C: Three Short Novels (2015)
The Atheist in the Attic (2018)

GRAPHIC NOVELS

Empire (artist, Howard Chaynkin, 1980)
Bread & Wine (artist, Mia Wolff, 1999)

THE JOURNALS OF SAMUEL R. DELANY (edited by Kenneth R. James)

Volume 1, 1957–1969
  In Search of Silence (2017)

NONFICTION

The Jewel-Hinged Jaw (1977; revised, 2008)
The American Shore (1978)
Heavenly Breakfast (1979)
Starboard Wine (1978; revised, 2008)
The Motion of Light in Water (1988)
Wagner/Artaud (1988)
The Straits of Messina (1990)
Silent Interviews (1994)
Longer Views (1996)
Times Square Red, Times Square Blue (1999)
Shorter Views (1999)
1984: Selected Letters (2000)
About Writing (2005)
Letters from Amherst (2019)
Occasional Views (2019)

Voyage, Orestes!

[a surviving novel fragment]

Samuel R. Delany

Bamberger Books
Whitmore Lake

Cover design and art: Ric Best

ISBN: 0-917453-44-1

Bamberger Books
Box 350
Whitmore Lake, MI 49189

To those
who wanted to see it
published.

CONTENTS

Introduction

By Kenneth R. James

Samuel R. Delany began writing *Voyage, Orestes!* — as he describes it, a "vast novel about poets, criminals, and folksingers loose in the streets of New York City" — at the Bread Loaf Writers' Conference in the summer of 1960, when he was eighteen years old.[1] He worked on the novel for the next three years. This period was eventful for young Delany, encompassing his brief stint at City College, the death of his father, the first years of his marriage to the poet Marilyn Hacker, several moves within New York City, and the beginning of his professional writing career. Delany finished the novel at his East Sixth Street apartment within an hour, one way or the other, of midnight on November 21, 1963 — the night before the assassination of President Kennedy.[2]

The completion of *Voyage, Orestes!* marked the culmination of a period of spectacular artistic productivity for Delany. While working on the book, he wrote and published

---

[1] Samuel R. Delany, "Ruins / Foundations," in *The Straits of Messina* (Seattle: Serconia Press, 1989), 116; *The Motion of Light in Water* (Minneapolis: University of Minnesota Press, 2004), 184.

[2] Personal communication with James, March 24, 2018. See also *Motion* 317-19.

five science fiction novels: *The Jewels of Aptor*, *The Ballad of Beta-2*, and the trilogy collectively titled *The Fall of the Towers*. Just before he married Hacker, Delany wrote three short non-science fiction novels: *The Flames of the Warthog*, *The Lovers*, and *The Assassination*.[3] None of the three was published, but *Warthog* lent its middle section to Chapter 8 of *Out of the Dead City*.

While still a student at the Bronx High School of Science, Delany had written five additional novels, also not science fiction.[4] Falling as it did at the end of this series of non-genre works, *Voyage, Orestes!*, with its 1,056 pages, its intertwining subplots, and its intricate orchestration of themes and devices, was to be a capstone piece, a summation of his non-SF writing up to that point.[5] Recalling the project twenty years later in his memoir *The Motion of Light in Water*, Delany describes it — in the second person, inviting the reader to imagine his experience — as "a novel in[to] which you have carefully cut and considered and organized and selected and placed — from your selections — everything important in your life."[6]

After the novel's completion, as Delany recounts in a draft of a letter of introduction to literary agent Henry Morrison written in 1965, *Voyage, Orestes!* went on to have a "jinxed

---

[3] Delany, *In Search of Silence*, ed. Kenneth R. James (Middletown, CT: Wesleyan University Press, 2017), 95.

[4] Delany, *Silence*, 1, 29. During this period Delany also wrote numerous short stories, plays, poems, translations, and songs.

[5] Delany, *Motion*, 317; personal communication with James, March 24, 2018.

[6] Ibid., 330; personal communication with James, March 24, 2018.

career."[7] In the letter Delany describes rejections from Appleton-Century-Crofts, Bobbs-Merrill, and Grove Press, garnished with dark details of editors committing suicide and entire fiction departments being cut. (In his personal journals from this period, Delany mentions another rejection from New American Library.[8]) Yet these rejections were happening in spite of very strong interest in Delany's work on the part of editors. Bobs Pinkerton at Appleton-Century-Crofts had been an enthusiastic supporter of *Voyage, Orestes!* while Delany was writing it. Barney Rosset at Grove Press — in a letter included after this introduction, to Bernard Kay, who was then acting as Delany's agent[9] — had acknowledged Delany's "great talent." And Margaret Marshall, an editor at Harcourt Brace, had, on the strength of another of Delany's submissions, arranged for his scholarship to Bread Loaf.[10] Why the difficulty, then? One answer is suggested in a remark Delany recalls from Marshall, later echoed by another editor in relation to *Voyage, Orestes!*, which conveys something of how American commercial publishers of the time conceived their own audiences: "Chip, you tell a good story. But, right now, there's a housewife somewhere in Nebraska, and we can't publish a first novel here unless there's something in it she can

---

[7] Delany, *Silence*, 324.

[8] Delany, *Silence*, 300, 301, 308.

[9] Eventually, Bernie Kay, Barney Rosset, Richard Seaver, and Delany all had lunch together to discuss the manuscript. Delany, e-mail correspondence with James, September 4, 2018.

[10] Delany, "Three, Two, One, Contact: Times Square Red," in *Times Square Red, Times Square Blue* (New York: New York University Press, 1999), 131.

relate to. And the fact is, there's *nothing* in your book she wants to know anything about at all. And that's probably why we *won't* publish it."[11]

After 1965 the jinx continued. Even as Delany's career as a science fiction writer blossomed, garnering him wide acclaim and, by 1968, three Nebula Awards, *Voyage, Orestes!* continued not to find a home. That same year, Morrison — who had by then become Delany's agent — notified him that during a relocation of his offices, a carton earmarked for manuscripts that had proven hard to place, which included a top copy of Delany's novel, had been lost. Upon learning this, Delany went to retrieve the other extant copy of the manuscript, in storage in the basement of the East Sixth Street apartment in which he'd lived a few years previously, only to learn that just six months earlier the building itself had been torn down.[12] Thus, unless an archeological dig beneath East Sixth Street turns something up, there is now *no* known surviving copy of the complete text of *Voyage, Orestes!* What remain are longhand drafts of portions of the novel in Delany's notebooks — short excerpts from which can be found in *In Search of Silence*, the first volume of his collected journals — and a typescript of the opening chapters, which Delany's friend Chris Terdsis had made while the novel was still in progress.[13] That typescript is the source of the fragment you now hold in your hands.

---

[11] Delany, "The Semiology of Silence," interview by Sinda Gregory and Larry McCaffery, in *Silent Interviews* (Middletown, CT: Wesleyan University Press, 1994), 43-4; *Motion,* 7-8, 328.

[12] Delany, *Motion*, 328-30.

[13] Delany, *Silence*, 199.

While the narrative material of *Voyage, Orestes!* was reorganized several times over the course of its writing (see Delany's working notes in *In Search of Silence*), the overall structure remained unchanged: a story in three parts, bracketed by a prologue and epilogue. The present fragment contains the opening paragraphs of the prologue, most of the three chapters that make up Part I ("The Road," "The Bridge," and "The City"), and the first chapter of Part II ("In Praise of Limestone"). There are two gaps within the fragment itself, which indicate places where Delany had extracted material from the typescript for use in other work: the bulk of the prologue, which served as the basis for the short story "Summer," and the opening eight sections of "The Road," which provided material for the short story "Tapestries."[14]

The prologue introduces the narrator, Jimmy Calvin, a black teenager hitchhiking through (then-) present-day New England. Jimmy has temporarily fled his home in Harlem, where his family is experiencing severe emotional strain due to his father's declining health. The first chapter of Part I, "The Road," cross-cuts between Jimmy's return to New York and his recollection, during his return, of the events that had led to his departure. At the chapter's climax, the moment of arrival and the remembered moment of departure converge; the circle closes and the chapter ends. However, because the opening sections of the chapter are missing, the reader must infer several episodes that have come before, which introduce a number of major and minor characters. After "The Road," the

---

[14] Delany, *Voyage, Orestes!*, typescript, Delany collection, Beinecke Rare Book & Manuscript Library, Yale University.

chapters move forward in unbroken succession, developing characters and introducing new ones, setting gears of plot and theme in motion, and concluding, neatly, with a second departure from the city. The sense of symmetry and closure here isn't simply fortuitous, but rather a function of Delany's careful, essentially musical arrangement of the narrative material. (Appropriately, the fragment ends in a moment of song.) As a result of his orchestration of incident, image, and theme, while the bulk of the novel is missing, what remains feels satisfying — feels, in its own way, whole.

Readers familiar with Delany's published fiction will find, among the novel's characters, prototypes for figures who will appear in Delany's later published work. Jimmy — traumatized, sharply observant, smarter than he lets on — anticipates similar troubled young witnesses like the Mouse (*Nova*) and Kid (*Dhalgren*). Jimmy's older friend Geo Keller, a gifted poet around whom a smog of fame has begun to gather, anticipates similarly brilliant, articulate, well-meaning and yet also vulnerable figures like Lump (*Empire Star*) and Katin (*Nova*). Together Jimmy and Geo perform the dialogue between observation and analysis — in James Sallis's characterization, the "commingling of sensation and intellect" — that contours much of Delany's published work.[15] The shadowy, erotic figure of Snake anticipates later figures like Denny (*Dhalgren*) and Shit (*Through the Valley of the Nest of Spiders*), and recalls his own namesake in *The Jewels of Aptor*, Delany's first published novel. (Two other major characters in

---

[15] James Sallis, introduction to *Ash of Stars: On the Writing of Samuel R. Delany*, ed. James Sallis (Jackson: University Press of Mississippi, 1996), xiv.

The Jewels of Aptor are named "Geo" and "Iimmi"; at one stage of the drafting of *Voyage, Orestes!*, Delany intended to embed *Jewels* inside the larger novel as a fiction-within-a-fiction.[16]) Additionally, Snake had been a "repeating dream figure" for Delany, as well as a persona he'd assumed while cruising in New York.[17] The folksinger Ann is a forerunner of several female artists — Rydra Wong (*Babel-17*), Lanya (*Dhalgren*), and the Spike (*Trouble on Triton*) — who are agents of mediation and integration, though in this novel the integrative role is itself split between Ann and Jimmy's sister, Margaret.[18] As for secondary players, the queer quasi-gang — some members of which we encounter at the party that commences the long night that makes up the bulk of Chapter III, the rest of whom appear later that same night, running among burning ruins like Dante's sodomites in the Seventh Circle — appears to be a prototype for the Singers in Delany's Hugo- and Nebula-winning short story "Time Considered as a Helix of Semi-Precious Stones," as well as the scorpions in *Dhalgren*. And O'Donnells, who appears at a second party on that same night in Chapter III, is a clear forerunner of various establishment figures who act, either unwittingly or with malice aforethought, as agents of control for the hegemonic official culture, such as Roger Calkins (*Dhalgren*), the schoolmaster of Kolhari (*Flight from Nevèrÿon*), and Irving Mossman (*The Mad Man*).

---

[16] Delany, *Silence*, 199-200.

[17] Delany, e-mail correspondence with James, April 19, 2018. See also *Motion* 134-141.

[18] "Margaret" was Delany's mother's name; Delany's actual, younger, sister is named Sara and nicknamed Peggy.

Readers of *The Motion of Light in Water* and other works by Delany involving memoir will recognize that many elements in the opening chapters of *Voyage, Orestes!* correspond closely to aspects of Delany's life during the period in which he wrote the novel. When Delany began developing *Voyage, Orestes!* at Bread Loaf, his own father was dying of lung cancer; sequences from both *Motion of Light in Water* and *In Search of Silence* suggest that the novel's account of Jimmy's experience of the decline and death of his father, as well as its aftermath, is a fairly direct transcription of Delany's experience.[19] The elegy that Geo improvises (or rather, seems to improvise) in response to Jimmy's father's death is a poem Delany had written hours after his own father's death, and indeed several other writings by Geo that Delany intended to place in the novel had been written by Delany on earlier occasions.[20] Geo's mentor, Bill Sloan, borrows his name from writer, editor, and publisher William Sloane, whom Delany had met at Bread Loaf; the character of Sloan was modeled after Delany's own mentor, Bernard Kay.[21] Geo's nickname for Jimmy, "Little Brother," had been Delany's nickname for a lover during his brief time at City College, as well as his nickname for Hacker.[22] The strained open marriage of Geo and Laile recalls Delany and Hacker's marriage during this time; more generally, both Jimmy and Geo's attempts to define and negotiate their own sexualities in the context of the hetero- and

---

[19] Delany, *Motion*, 3-6.

[20] Delany, *Motion*, 5; *Silence*, 104-5, 134-5.

[21] Delany, "Three, Two, One, Contact: Times Square Red," 131; personal communication with James, March 24, 2018.

[22] Delany, *Motion*, 9; personal communication with James, March 24, 2018.

homosexual relationships each engages in (though these narrative threads are not clearly established and developed until later in the novel) reflect Delany's own struggles.[23] (Even without knowing the biographical particulars, most readers will discern that Jimmy and Geo are younger and older versions of the same person.[24]) The circulation of the various characters through New York's bohemian and literary scene echoes Delany's own youthful experiences as a precocious and prize-winning writer during and shortly after high school, as well as his experiences among the students and professors who were Hacker's peers and instructors at New York University.[25] Finally, the increasing importance of music, particularly folk music, over the course of the story reflects Delany's own involvement in the American folk revival of the time, starting with his youthful experiences at the progressive and music-oriented Camp Woodland in the '50s; over the course of the subsequent decade, Delany performed variously as a solo singer-songwriter, as a member of a folk group he'd co-founded, The Harbor Singers, and, later, as a member of the

---

[23] Various working notes for the novel in *In Search of Silence*, like the one presented later in this essay, hint at these narrative developments. As for the women in these relationships, Delany has indicated in correspondence that Laile ultimately ends up leaving Geo "for good," while Ann, contrariwise, declares that she is "comfortable with [Jimmy's] multiple sexualities" (Delany, e-mail to James, April 19, 2018).

[24] Delany has confirmed this in correspondence: "Geo was basically me after I married. Jimmy was me before I married." Delany, e-mail to James, April 19, 2018.

[25] Delany, *Silence*, xvii, 1, 608-10; *Motion* 95, 98-9.

folk-rock group Heavenly Breakfast.[26]

Embracing all of the characters and events of the novel, whether autobiographically grounded or otherwise, is New York City, that vast urban landscape which will reflect and refract throughout Delany's later work. Delany's New York is a generous city, a city of near-infinite possibility — including, it should be said, the possibility of violence, though as Delany suggests in *Voyage, Orestes!* and later work, such violence is far more likely to strike from the hegemonic center — or better, in the *name* of such a center, whether it exists or not — than from the criminal margins. Although the opening chapters of *Voyage, Orestes!* only begin to treat this narrative thread, Geo Keller is very much a city poet; in Delany's recollection of the novel, Geo's major work, a "book-length poem" entitled *The Fall of the Towers*, was "envisioned as something between Eliot's *The Waste Land* and Crane's *The Bridge*."[27] (As mentioned earlier, *The Fall of the Towers* was also the collective title of the SF trilogy Delany wrote at the same time as *Voyage, Orestes!* Delany explains in *Motion* — and explains again in *Voyage, Orestes!* through the mouth of Geo, in another moment of near-direct autobiography — that the title had originally designated a series of drawings by Cary Reinstein, a friend of Delany's from Bronx Science. Delany appropriated the title to commemorate the drawings after Reinstein's mother, in a bid to dissuade Reinstein from pursuing an artistic career and push him toward bourgeois "security," threw them

---

[26] Delany, *Motion*, 44-46, 99, 296-9; *Silence*, 172-7. See also *Heavenly Breakfast: An Essay on the Winter of Love* (1979. Reprint. Flint, Michigan: Bamberger Books, 1997).

[27] Delany, *Motion*, 184.

down her apartment building's incinerator chute, along with Reinstein's other drawings and writings.[28] In the name of the center, violence.)

The various areas of New York in which the bulk of the drama of *Voyage, Orestes!* plays out have specific correlates in Delany's own life. Delany was raised in a three-story house at 2250 Seventh Avenue in Harlem.[29] In 1957 his family moved to 80 LaSalle Street in the Morningside Gardens housing cooperative, just north of Columbia University; it was here that Delany did his earliest work on *Voyage, Orestes!*[30] Shortly after the start of his first term at City College, and his father's death, in the fall of 1960, Delany moved into the apartment of his neighbor Bob Aarenberg at the St.-Marks Arms building on West 113th Street.[31] Immediately after Delany and Hacker were married in August 1961, they moved into a 2nd floor apartment at 629 East Fifth Street, and in spring 1963 they moved to a 4th floor apartment at 739 East Sixth Street, which their friend Rose Marion was vacating; it was at the latter apartment that Delany finished *Voyage, Orestes!* as well as the *Fall of the Towers* trilogy, and from there that Delany eventually departed for his travels in Europe.[32]

---

[28] Ibid., 197-9.

[29] Michael W. Peplow and Robert S. Bravard, *Samuel R. Delany: A Primary and Secondary Bibliography* (Boston: G. K. Hall & Co., 1980), 3; Delany, e-mail to James, June 2, 2018.

[30] Delany (as K. Leslie Steiner), "Samuel R. Delany," *Pseudopodium*, Ray Davis, https://www.pseudopodium.org/repress/KLeslieSteiner-SamuelRDelany.html

[31] Delany, *Motion*, 8.

[32] Ibid., 13, 19-20, 301, 317.

New York City as it appears in *Voyage, Orestes!* recalls other cities in literary works Delany was familiar with at the time. It carries overtones of the simultaneously romantic and alienating Paris of Hemingway and Miller, as well as the Paris of Gide's *Les Faux-monnayeurs*, with its intersecting circles of students, writers, homosexuals, and criminals — not to mention that novel's intricate interplay of text and embedded text.[33] It also recalls Durrell's Alexandria, which, similar to Gide's Paris, is a landscape of language in motion.[34] Like those fictional cities — and indeed like Delany's own later fanciful cities of Bellona and Kolhari — New York City in *Voyage, Orestes!* is an arena for the circulation of people and discourse, as well as the transformation of one into the other; characters appear first as figures of rumor and gossip before they arrive onstage, and then dissolve back into the social matrix in the form of the stories and legends, the myths, that they leave behind.

And myth is the central concern of *Voyage, Orestes!*; it is the master-concept that binds together the novel's many narrative and thematic strands. Delany discusses this concept in his letter to Morrison:

> [*Voyage, Orestes!*] takes a young man, 19, through a series of interlocking adventures the subject of which is the conflict between the myths of society concerning Negroes, Artists, and Women. The myths dealt with, however, are not the nineteenth century ones which

---

[33] Delany, *Silence*, 147, 211, 217, 281.

[34] Ibid., 121, 147.

> have been poked and punched to death. But rather the contemporary ones that I had to come to terms with to deal with the world.[35]

One of the most salient aspects of the world of American society at the time, and its myths, was, of course, that both were undergoing, or about to undergo, explosive change. Delany began writing *Voyage, Orestes!* just after the passage of the Civil Rights Act of 1960, and completed it eight months before the passage of the Civil Rights Act of 1964. Completion also came just before the earliest public expressions of both second wave feminism and the antiwar movement, both of which would coalesce over the remainder of the decade. And at the decade's end would come the Stonewall riots. The period just before, during and after the writing of the novel would be marked by the upending of entrenched political, social and cultural orthodoxies — by "mythoclasm," to use Roland Barthes' term — on a grand scale.

The science fiction works Delany had already produced and would continue to produce over the remainder of the decade — *Babel-17*, *Empire Star*, *The Einstein Intersection*, *Nova*, and a handful of short stories — would address many of the social and mythical transformations of the era. But *Voyage, Orestes!* was written at the leading edge of those changes, and in the mode of literary realism, not SF. How does the novel handle its mythical material differently from Delany's SF of the time?

A hint of an answer is suggested by the contrasting ways *Voyage, Orestes!* and *The Fall of the Towers* (again, written

[35] Ibid., 324.

contemporaneously with one another) represent their respective urban landscapes. In the former work, while the narrative action occasionally takes us elsewhere, the landscape of interest is, specifically and centrally, New York, in all its myriad particulars. In the latter, the landscape of interest is, ostensibly, also a single city: Toron, a far-future metropolis on a post-apocalyptic Earth. However, from the very start of the trilogy, Toron is juxtaposed with other cities and considered in relation to them. Before we encounter Toron, we are given a glimpse of Telphar, a radioactive ruin. The fate of this city haunts the major characters of the trilogy; it is a city of the past, utterly destroyed. Later, near the trilogy's close, several of these characters arrive at the City of a Thousand Suns, a utopian city of the future, still under construction. And at other moments in the narrative, through a form of telepathic projection, the characters are able to traverse space and mentally inhabit an alien city, which, in turn, is shown to exist in a state of superimposition with a variety of other cities throughout the galaxy. Thus the trilogy expands the narrative frame to encompass all possible cities, the city in general. Indeed, the final novel in the trilogy opens with a meditation on the general question: "What is a city?"[36]

This basic contrast between particularity and generality is central to one of Delany's very earliest critical writings on SF, produced just a few years after he'd completed *Voyage, Orestes!* and *The Fall of the Towers*. In the piece, which was eventually published in truncated form in *New Worlds*, Delany

---

[36] Delany, *The Fall of the Towers* (1966. Reprint. New York: Bantam, 2004), 295.

suggests that the proper fictive object of SF is "theory" (of society, mind, communication, and so on) and that the tropes of SF, such as aliens or telepathy, serve to concretize theoretical notions.[37] By way of example, Delany notes that Norman Mailer's *The Naked and the Dead* makes a "statement about a real war," while Heinlein's *Starship Troopers* makes "an abstract statement about a theory behind war."[38] (Delany's mention of *Starship Troopers* here is significant, as he has claimed that he'd conceived *The Fall of the Towers* in part as a science-fictional response to that novel.[39]) Applying this distinction to *Voyage, Orestes!* and *The Fall of the Towers*, we can read the two works together as, among other things, a dialogue between New York City and its theory. (Whether the theory is *adequate* to the city is another question; Delany has, in hindsight, been quite critical of the conceptual framework of *The Fall of the Towers*.[40])

In his later critical writings Delany would explore deeply the distinctions between SF and "mundane" fiction, characterizing these genres as language-like entities, as discourses — sets of protocols by means of which readers make sense of texts.[41] For Delany, a key difference between the two discourses, as 20th (and now 21st) century readers have inherited them, lies in the role played by the fictive "world" in

---

37 Delany, *Silence*, 371.

38 Ibid., 370.

39 Ibid., 519.

40 Delany, *Motion*, 306-7.

41 Delany, "Science Fiction and Literature — or, the Conscience of the King," in *Starboard Wine* (1984. Reprint. Middletown, CT: Wesleyan University Press, 2012), 68.

each — with the notion of "world" construed not in terms of some nebulous notion of narrative content, but rather in terms of the readerly effects it generates. In a work of mundane fiction, the narrative plays out against a world we are to take as correlating to a given, consensus view of reality, and this produces a particular sort of reading experience:

> Because in the discourse of mundane fiction the world is a given, you must use each sentence in a mundane fiction text as part of a sort of hunt-and-peck game: All right, what part of the world must I summon up in my imagination to pay attention to (and, equally, what other parts — especially as sentences build up — and I best not pay attention to it all) if I want this story to hang together?[42]

The fixedness of the world in mundane fiction organizes the reading protocols of this form around what Delany calls "subject priority" — a directing of the reader's attention toward individual psychology and action, with the "stabilia" of the given world serving as readerly anchor-points.[43] (Delany adds: "I say 'given world' rather than 'real world' because the world of the most naturalistic piece of mundane fiction is a highly conventionalized affair; and these conventions, when one studies them, turn out to have far more to do with other

---

[42] Ibid., 69, 140-2.

[43] Delany, *The American Shore*, 28-9.

works of fiction than with anything 'real.'[44]) An SF story, however, adds a new term to the narrative equation:

> In science fiction the world of the story is not a given, but rather a construct that changes from story to story. To read an SF text, we have to indulge a much more fluid and speculative kind of game. With each sentence we have to ask what in the world of the tale would have to be different from our world for such a sentence to be uttered — and thus, as the sentences build up, we build up a world in specific dialogue, in a specific tension, with our present concept of the real.[45]

The unfixed nature of the world in any given work of SF organizes the reading protocols of the form around "object priority" – a directing of the reader's attention toward context or situation, with situation treated from the start as an open variable which acquires value and resonance as the reading proceeds.[46]

These earlier and later formulations seem to differ in where they locate the site of the abstraction process in SF: in the earlier, it resides in the story's theme, its argument; in the later, in the reader's act of interpretation. This may account for the rather schematic quality of the *Fall of the Towers* trilogy as compared to, say, *Nova*, written a few years later — whose science fictional world, just as unreal as that of the trilogy,

---

[44] Delany, "Some Presumptuous Approaches to Science Fiction," in *Starboard Wine*, 29.

[45] Ibid., 69.

[46] Ibid., 140-2.

unfolds in a cascade of vivid particulars, by means of which the reader, through a host of cognitive moves (inference, induction, deduction, analogy…), constructs his or her mental model of it. Moreover, in mapping that model onto the real world, the reader must engage in further abstraction and attend to what aspects the particulars of the two worlds do or do not share — that is, to what in them is conceptual, structural.

Some remarks by Delany from several decades after these early critical formulations — in a roundtable discussion on politics in literature — make this point vividly, and suggest the basic continuity of Delany's concerns between his earlier and later critical work:

> … in my own recent [Nevèrÿon] stories, it should slowly creep up on most readers that the barbarians, who have just come to the city and are creating so many social problems, are blond and blue-eyed while the ordinary citizens are dark. What is actually gained by this kind of reversal — the dark-skinned citizens learning to live with and/or ignore the blond-haired barbarians, in, say, the equivalent of a pre-historic bus terminal as if the barbarians weren't there (like middle-class New Yorkers ignoring the many people who hang out or even live in the Port Authority Station) — is that it distances the situation. At the same time, one recognizes it as the structure rather than as the *content* of the way black people act or the way white people act. It shows the way people who are in a certain relationship to each other, whether they are black or white, act… [I]f you're directly writing about the black

> situation, you use this experience directly. But if you are writing in a figurative form, as I am with science fiction, what you have to do is tease out the structure of the situation, move on one step down the line of analysis, and replace the experiential terms with the new and opaque terms that are appropriate to the figure. Hopefully the structures that you first saw remain recognizable.[47]

The protocols of mundane fiction invite the reader to attend to character and action as they play out in the arena of the fixed, particularized real; those of science fiction invite the reader to attend to the entire fictive landscape in specifically *structural* counterpoint to the real. To float a mathematical metaphor: if mundane fiction directs our attention to the arithmetic of the world, science fiction directs our attention to its algebra.

If we grant the distinction between the two forms as Delany characterizes it in these later essays, this suggests that if *Voyage, Orestes!* is concerned with myth, then as a realist novel, it must capture, with vividness and precision, the "arithmetic" of myth. In terms of Delany's own stated intentions, it must capture the arithmetic of the mythic figures he names in his letter to Morrison — "Women," "Negroes," and "Artists" — as he encountered them in the early '60s. Without actually assessing his success — I leave that to the reader — I'll briefly present some observations by Delany

[47] Delany, contribution to "Forum: Writing and Politics," in *Fiction International* 15:1, 1984, 11-13. In the cited paragraph, "Nevèrÿon" is written without diacritical marks; I have presented the correct form in brackets.

himself on the circumstances of his life during the time he composed the novel, which suggest some of what was at stake for Delany as he grappled with these myths in the arena of literary realism.

In the first year of Delany's marriage, the experiences of Hacker and her friends as they began to negotiate the professional world became part of the texture of Delany's own daily experience:

> The women friends who dropped by our Lower East Side Apartment that year seemed to have only one topic of conversation. Most of them were Marilyn's university friends, and they were all moving from the world of the university and home to the world of work and self-sufficiency. The most frequent topic of conversation was:
>
> What do you do about jobs that advertised positions as "editors," "travel agents," or "stock brokers" in the women's classified section of the *Times* and that closed with the phrase: "Some typing required." The inclusion of this phrase, all these young women had found out, meant that, regardless of the title of the job, you were going to be somebody's secretary.
>
> They didn't want to be secretaries.
>
> They had just completed university.
>
> They wanted to be editors, travel agents, stockbrokers.
>
> I must have sat and listened to hundreds of hours of conversation in which these young women tried to figure out strategies for how to deal with this.

> [...] Yet this was women's talk — and as such was as outside the parameters of language as was the sex I indulged in.[48]

Delany's first literary attempts to address the exclusion of women from economic power, and their experiences from official language, were instigated primarily by Hacker, who *had* managed to land a job as an editorial assistant, at the science fiction publisher, Ace Books. Her reports of her experiences at the offices of Ace — where the submissions in the editorial slush pile consistently featured poorly drawn female characters — galvanized Delany, who wrote *The Jewels of Aptor* in part as a response to that situation.[49]

In *Motion*, Delany describes discussing problems of gender representation with Hacker in relation to his next SF project, *The Fall of the Towers*; as the following passage suggests, both he and Hacker recognized that these problems extended well beyond science fiction:

> Among the conclusions we reached... was that for a novel, SF or otherwise, to show any aesthetic originality in the range of extant American fiction, it must portray, among many other sorts of relationships, at least one strong friendship between two women characters. Also, the major heterosexual relationship had to involve a woman as active as the man. [...] Both

---

[48] Delany, *Motion*, 189-90.

[49] Delany, *Motion*, 150-1.

> characters must be developed as human beings, we decided, before they hooked up. [50]

A little over a decade later, in his contribution to the 1975 *Khatru* Symposium on Women in Science Fiction, Delany would state one of the above rules of thumb as follows: "Women characters must have central-to-the-plot, strong, developing, positive relations with other women characters."[51] (A decade further on, a version of this rule would become famous as the "Bechdel Test," named for its appearance in Alison Bechdel's comic strip *Dykes to Watch Out For*. In considering the historical precedents for the Test, Duncan Mitchel notes that in addition to Delany, Virginia Woolf had arrived at a similar formulation in *A Room of One's Own*; Bechdel herself, who had first heard the rule from her friend Liz Wallace, speculates that Wallace had gotten the rule from Woolf.[52])

As for how this concern manifests in *Voyage, Orestes!*, we note that in the opening chapters, while Jimmy discusses Geo Keller's mythical status directly — as a sensitive observer of a figure of legend, Jimmy is Nick Carraway to Geo's Gatsby — perhaps the most conspicuous mythical figure in these chapters

---

[50] Ibid., 189.

[51] Delany, "Letter to the Symposium on 'Women in Science Fiction,' Under the Control, for Some Deeply Suspect Reason, of One Jeff Smith," in *The Jewel-Hinged Jaw* (1978. Revised edition. Middletown, CT: Wesleyan University Press, 2009), 102.

[52] Duncan Mitchel, "The Rule," *This Is So Gay,* http://thisislikesogay.blogspot.com/2009/10/rule.html; Alison Bechdel, "Testy," *Alison Bechdel* (blog), November 8, 2013, http://dykestowatchoutfor.com/testy.

is Geo's estranged wife Laile. Laile remains offstage throughout, yet is powerfully present as a topic of discussion and speculation. Her absence as subject and presence as mythical object suggests a response on Delany's part both to the situation of women and to the problem of addressing this in literary discourse, the male domination of which Delany, and his fictive mouthpieces, participates in. Even as Geo indicates his awareness of the situation of women to Jimmy early in the novel, Laile's absence from the stage renders all his formulations suspect: Geo still occupies the spotlight, commands the discourse. Another passage from Delany's journals, intended to be inserted in this scene (whether it made it into the final manuscript, we cannot now know), dramatizes the problem:

> Geo began a philippic on the problems of Modern Women. It held me by its wit. I goaded him, taking everything he offered as revolutionary and pointed out how old-fashioned it was. Goad him it did. We amused ourselves like for blocks, till it struck me that the inspiration for all this wit was sitting alone back in his apartment. The whole business suddenly seemed rather empty.[53]

Laile does eventually appear later in the novel; we simply don't have access to those chapters. But the chapters we do have establish a plot thread that will run through much of the remainder of the narrative: a search for a missing woman. And

---

[53] Delany, *Silence*, 534.

this search will reveal the mechanics of the myth. By demarcating the literary negative space, the x-variable position that Laile eventually arrives to occupy, *Voyage, Orestes!* attempts in realist terms what a science fiction novel might attempt by other means.

In considering the angle of approach *Voyage, Orestes!* takes to myths of "Negroes," it is useful to recall Delany's personal background as part of a very accomplished African-American family. His grandfather, Henry Beard Delany, had been born into slavery, but following its abolition had grown up to become vice-principal of St. Augustine's College in North Carolina, as well as the first African-American elected suffragan bishop of the Episcopal Church in the United States. The elder Delany's children distinguished themselves in many ways; Samuel Delany's own father, Samuel Ray Delany Sr., was a successful funeral director in Harlem. Delany's mother, Margaret Carey Boyd Delany, worked for the New York Public Library system.[54] Two of Delany's uncles on each side of the family, Hubert Delany and Myles Paige, were judges as well as important civil rights activists in New York City, and the entire extended family was politically sophisticated and active.[55] Yet all this achievement and relative affluence was situated within the larger context of a United States where the advances of the Civil Rights movement were still underway. In relation to this context, the class position of Delany's family was an

---

[54] Delany, personal communication with James, March 24, 2018; Peplow and Bravard, 2.

[55] Peplow and Bravard, 3-4; Martha Biondi, *To Stand and Fight: The Struggle for Postwar Civil Rights in New York City* (Cambridge, MA: Harvard University Press, 2003), 40, 216-17, 253.

ambiguous thing; Delany has mentioned that the publication in 1957 of E. Franklin Frazier's *Black Bourgeoisie*, which sharply questioned the meaning of middle-class identity in the black community at the time, had prompted much debate in his extended family.[56] The reader might consider this background and context in relation to the images *Voyage, Orestes!* presents of black middle-class life: its social phenomenology and its structures of feeling, its moments of communion and its schismatic silences.

In relation to the literary givens of the day, consider how the larger context of ongoing social upheaval impinged on Delany's experiences as a young reader of African American writers. Delany recalls some of these experiences in his essay "The Necessity of Tomorrow(s)," based on a talk delivered in 1978 at the Studio Museum in Harlem:

> … I read James Baldwin's early essays that were to be first collected in *Notes of a Native Son*, and I thought they were as wonderful as… Well, as science fiction. I also read Richard Wright's *Black Boy* and Chester Himes's *If He Hollers Let Him Go*, and they seemed… well, history. They certainly didn't take place in the world of freedom marches and integration rallies. Did they explain them? They certainly said that the condition of the black man in America was awful — somehow the black woman in these fictive endeavors

[56] James, introduction to *In Search of* Silence, xxxvi. Frazier was also part of the extended Delany family by marriage; he was the husband of Delany's uncle Lemuel's wife's sister (Delany, personal communication with James, March 24, 2018).

> got mysteriously shortchanged in a manner suspiciously similar to the way the white woman was getting shortchanged in the work of Wright's and Himes's white male contemporaries. (The black woman was somehow always the cause *and* the victim at once of everything that went wrong with the black man.) But Wright and Himes seem to say as well that, in any realistic terms, precisely what made it so awful also made it unchangeable. And they said it with a certainty that, to me, dwarfed the moments of interracial rapprochement one found in books like John O. Killens's *Youngblood*, no matter how much more pleasant Killens might have been for us youngsters to read. One began to suspect that it was precisely the certainty that no real change was possible that had made Wright and Hines as popular as they were with those strangely always absent readers who establish books as classics. At least that's what I seemed to read in them in a world that was clearly exploding with racial change from headline to headline.[57]

Later, while Delany was completing *Voyage, Orestes!*, Baldwin's novel *Another Country* was published. Like Delany's work in progress, *Another Country* examined American racial politics through the lens of interracial friendships and sexual relationships — hetero-, bi-, and homosexual. Delany's response to the novel, at the time, was decidedly negative:

---

[57] Delany, "The Necessity of Tomorrows," in *Starboard Wine*, 6-7.

> I hated the book.
>
> I thought it was a bad, sloppy, unstructured novel. (I am much less vehement about its flaws today.) It was about everything in my life (sex, death, race, art…). But instead of proffering the reassuring message that it is the novel's mandate to offer the young (however chaotic it looks, this life-material is negotiable and though the life-contradictions it engenders may wreak death and havoc among these or those major or minor characters caught up in a subplot, the true hero, through knowledge, strength, and grace, can still prevail…), *this* novel shrieked and gibbered and babbled banalities and sobbed and rambled and screamed, and screamed, and *screamed* in all modes of awe and terror before life's mystery, wonder, and horror. In short, it dramatized in its form, through however distorted a manner, a truth. It just wasn't a truth I needed, right then and there, to hear.[58]

For Delany, the proper aesthetic approach to the racial complexities of the day "was not to slough off form, but to invent/reformulate a new one."[59]

Science fiction, with its alternative landscapes, offered one kind of formal solution. Published later in the decade, Delany's novels *Babel-17* and *Nova* feature starship captain-protagonists

---

[58] Delany, "An Interview with Samuel R. Delany," interview by Charles H. Rowell, in *Conversations with Samuel R. Delany*, ed. Carl Freedman (Jackson: University Press of Mississippi, 2009), 33-4.

[59] Ibid., 35.

who are, respectively, an Asian woman and a black man; these SF novels straightforwardly change the "object" and install people of color in positions of authority. However, when Delany submitted *Nova* to editor John W. Campbell for serialization in the science fiction magazine *Analog*, he met with resistance similar in form to that met by *Voyage, Orestes!* As Delany recounts, Campbell rejected the book "not because he was bothered by the fact that my main character was black, but because he was sure his readers would be — readers who, incidentally, once the book was published a year later, kept the book in print for the next twenty-five years."[60] Having proffered a new image — the black male SF protagonist — Delany was met with a counter-image: the hypothetical reader who could not accept such a protagonist. The manner in which both *Voyage, Orestes!* and *Nova* were submitted for and blocked from publication anticipates later novels by Delany — *Dhalgren*, the Nevèrÿon books, *Stars in My Pocket Like Grains of Sand* — which portray social struggles in which images and counter-images, myths and counter-myths, are potent political weapons.

Meanwhile, how to address the same complexities through the "subject"-oriented protocols of mundane fiction? If *Another Country* dramatizes, among other things, the decline and defeat of one of its principal characters, Rufus Scott, under the pressure of internalized racial and sexual violence, how does *Voyage, Orestes!* present a more optimistic vision and carve out a space for a black subject who can "prevail"?

---

[60] Delany, "Pornography and Censorship," in *Shorter Views* (Middletown, CT: Wesleyan University Press, 1999), 296.

One answer to this question might be that it approaches that subject in a partially science-fictional manner, by dramatizing the manifold ways in which, in Delany's phrasing, "the subject [is] excited, impinged on, contoured and constituted by the object."[61] Certainly one of the most arresting features of *Voyage, Orestes!*, for this reader at any rate, is its portrayal of the way New York City impinges on Jimmy's consciousness; like a jewel turning steadily in light, the city continually presents a new facet to Jimmy, a new configuration, in moment after moment of cleansing lucidity. In this sense the urban landscape of *Voyage, Orestes!* recalls that of Crane's poem *The Bridge* as Delany characterizes it in his extended essay, "Atlantis Rose…": "…Crane's poem limns a world where not only the Poet, but every element of it, can apostrophize — can directly address — every other."[62] In *Voyage, Orestes!* the city constantly apostrophizes Jimmy; the novel's title itself can be taken as an apostrophe. But this hailing from the object is only part of the story; the novel also examines and affirms the resources of the subject, the energies the subject can bring to bear on the object in order to open itself up to it. Note, for instance, the circuitous journey of Margaret's green scarf in Chapter III, as it passes from character to character like a baton, now alighting on this character, now on the next, signifying Margaret's generous, inclusive attention. This attention, a source of power and grace, extends beyond the bounds of the narrative itself, attributable not just to Margaret,

---

[61] Delany, "*Dichtung und* Science Fiction," in *Starboard Wine* (1984. Reprint. Middletown, CT: Wesleyan University Press, 2012), 178.

[62] Delany, "Atlantis Rose…," in *Longer Views* (Middletown, CT: Wesleyan University Press, 1996), 246.

but, at its origin, to her author, and, at the moment of reading, to the reader.

Which brings us to myths of "Artists." Delany's science fiction from the period during and after the composition of *Voyage, Orestes!* was much occupied with the mythical figure of the precocious young artist, or criminal-artist, after the model of Arthur Rimbaud; think of Vol Nonik, Rydra Wong, or Ni Ty Lee. In *Voyage, Orestes!*, Geo Keller obviously exemplifies this sort of figure. But in his letter to Morrison discussing the publication woes of *Voyage, Orestes!*, Delany says in passing, "[The novel] has gone to Grove Press, but it is simply not their sort of book and jumps up and down on the toes of the monsters off whom they make their living — with track shoes."[63] Yet the writers championed by Grove at that time, such as Miller, Burroughs, Genet, and other figures — artists with whose work Delany was deeply engaged — exemplified the Rimbaldian type.[64] What is the nature of the critique of this artistic type that Delany suggests his novel makes?

An answer to *this* question is suggested by a statement — or better, the context of a statement — that the character Lump offers to the protagonist Comet Jo in *Empire Star*: "The only important elements in any society are the artistic and the criminal, because they alone, by questioning the society's values, can force it to change."[65] What complicates this somewhat pat claim is that Lump, using his far-future society's

---

[63] Delany, *Silence*, 35.

[64] Delany, *Motion*, 195.

[65] Delany, *Empire Star* (1966. Reprint. New York: Vintage Books, 2001), 74-75.

intellectual rubric of "simplex / complex / multiplex" perspectives, characterizes the statement as itself (only) "complex," and requiring further "multiplex evaluation."[66] And in fact the entire surrounding narrative provides the context that complicates the implications of the statement: the vast interstellar society and the intricate time-looping that weaves together its history render the clean divisions implied by the statement — between social insider and social outsider, individual and collective change, personal and historical narrative — porous and fluid. In such a context — in such a situation of the "object" — the mythic figure of the criminal-artist begins to complicate, ramify, disintegrate. Another answer is suggested by the model of the subject proffered by Rimbaud himself in his letter to Georges Izambard in 1871: "...I have realized that I am a poet. It's not my doing at all. It's wrong to say: I think. Better to say: I am thought... *I* is an *other*."[67] This split subject, differing from himself, half-inside and half-outside his own language, will become an increasingly important in Delany's work from *Dhalgren* on; much of his subsequent fiction and nonfiction will examine this split or sundered subject in specifically Lacanian terms.

---

[66] Ibid., 74. Delany has subsequently noted that the conceptual framework "simplex / complex / multiplex" can itself be deconstructed; to express this somewhat paradoxically, such a framework can only be a "complex" notion at best (Delany, "The Wiggle Room of Theory: An Interview with Samuel R. Delany," interview by Josh Lukin, in *Conversations with Samuel R. Delany*, 172-4).

[67] Arthur Rimbaud, *Arthur Rimbaud: Complete Works*, trans. Paul Schmidt (New York: HarperCollins Publishers, 2000), 113.

How are these outer fluidities and inner splits dramatized by the situation of Geo Keller? With this question, the consideration of myths of "Artists" in *Voyage, Orestes!* begins to converge with the consideration of a group that is conspicuously — and in those pre-Stonewall days, probably strategically — not named in Delany's letter to Morrison: "Homosexuals." We know from Delany's essays, journals, and memoirs that by the time he began drafting *Voyage, Orestes!* he was familiar with the homosexual literary tradition, from ancient Greco-Roman (Sappho, Petronius) to modern and then-contemporary French (Rimbaud, Proust, Gide, Cocteau, Genet) to American (verse by Whitman, Crane and Auden, prose by Barnes, Baldwin, Vidal, and Rechy).[68] At its very opening, *Voyage, Orestes!* confidently positions itself in relation to this tradition: the first paragraph turns on the word "sextillions" — a nod to Whitman's "Song of Myself," which is peppered with names for very large numbers (millions, trillions, quadrillions, quintillions, sextillions, decillions) to convey its multifarious, cosmic perspective.[69] But, analogously with his readings of the African-American writers of the day, a notable feature of this literature for Delany — particularly the literature produced in the United States around the time he was drafting the novel — was the divergence between what it proclaimed and Delany's own lived experience as a young gay man. The public image, the myth, of homosexuality promulgated in the literature of that pre-Stonewall period conveyed an unmistakable message:

---

[68] *Silence* 9, 34, 46, *Motion* 102, 162-3, 194.

[69] Walt Whitman, "Song of Myself," in *Leaves of Grass and Other Writings: A Norton Critical Edition*, ed. Michael Moon (New York: W. W. Norton & Company, 2002), 26-78. See editor's footnote, 27.

> In the 50s — and it was a 50s model of homosexuality that controlled all that was done, both by ourselves and the law that persecuted us — homosexuality was a solitary perversion. Before and above all, it isolated you.[70]

Delany's experiences, however, "flew in the face of that whole 50s image."[71] Recalling his first encounter with the St. Marks baths, as well as his witnessing of the sudden simultaneous appearance of hundreds of men as they fled from a police raid on a cruising enclave on Christopher Street, Delany describes how "the apprehension of massed bodies" in both of these moments suggested a situation at sharp variance with the myth of the isolated homosexual:

> …what this experience said was that there was a population — not of individual homosexuals, some of whom now and then encountered, or that those encounters could be human and fulfilling in their way — not of hundreds, not of thousands, but rather of millions of gay men, and that history had, actively and already, created for us whole galleries of institutions, good and bad, to accommodate our sex.[72]

The magnitude of this departure from the myth "was frightening to those of us who'd had no suggestion of it before

---

[70] Delany, *Motion*, 292.

[71] Ibid., 292.

[72] Ibid., 293.

— no matter how sophisticated our literary encounters with Petronius and Gide."[73] In relation to Delany's experience of the rupture between mythical image and lived reality, we note that when queerness first appears directly and forcefully in *Voyage, Orestes!*, it does so in the person of Daniele and her friends — does so, that is, not with the image of a solitary figure but with that of a group. To move in the direction of one's desire is not to depart from society, but rather to approach another sector within it. As Delany would remark thirty years later about urban spaces catering to sexual needs — analogous to the St. Marks baths — "Such institutions are always already within the social; indeed they *are* the social — and are not outside it."[74]

Various of Delany's working notes for the novel suggest that the disjunction between public myth and lived reality in relation to sexual practice was intended to manifest throughout the narrative, both in its smaller interpersonal moments and larger plot developments. In one note — a short passage intended to be inserted in a later sequence in the novel, by which point the relationships between Jimmy, Geo, and Snake have become sexual — intimacy and eroticism are articulated in terms of the divergence between expectation and reality:

> From our own encounters, I had somehow assumed that all Geo's sex with men was masochistic, or at least violent. But Snake (his shirt slipped to the floor) turned toward Geo who with his hands on the boy's face,

[73] Ibid., 293.

[74] Delany, "Three, Two, One, Contact: Times Square Red," in *Times Square Red, Times Square Blue*, 198.

> pressed his cheek against the mute face; and firmly his hands moved over the taut small muscles of the back, darker than his fingers. And a steady, quiet rhythm took over their two bodies. I went into the kitchen.[75]

Meanwhile, other notes indicate that all around these moments of sexual contact and possibility, the mechanism of myth continues to do its work — and in one part of that mechanism the gears of "Homosexual" and "Artist" are tightly meshed. One such note describes some of the elements of the "Artist" myth that coalesces around Geo over the course of the novel:

> <u>Growth of Legend</u>
>
> The publicity, magazine use, etc.
>
> Was he really a hero, just walk[ed] into it
>
> Need of child prodigy.
>
> […]
>
> Old poems vs. new work
>
> Homosexual or not[76]

---

[75] Delany, *Silence*, 241. The speaker is Jimmy.

[76] Delany, *Silence*, 240. These working notes are presented with some elisions (indicated by ellipses) to maintain clarity and avoid certain spoilers. The reader is invited to examine the fuller selection of notes in *In Search of Silence*.

But to what use does Geo's society put these "mythemes"? Here we recall a remark by Delany on the politics of literary reputation:

> The careful analysis of a public success, however small that public, is always instructive. But by the same token, accepting public opinion as an essential given of one's analytic matrix, as one explores a public success or a public failure, always hinders insight, because public opinions are myths — and myths, as Cassirer and others have noted, are invariably conservative "if only through the committee nature of their composition." [77]

In *Voyage, Orestes!*, the stance of uncritical acceptance and promulgation of public opinion, of myth, is represented by O'Donnells. How Delany intended to develop O'Donnells' role later in the novel is suggested by another working note concerning O'Donnells' intention to write a literary biography of Geo, which gives Geo's ambiguous sexuality, as well as the other complexities in his life, a fixed — and hugely distorted — meaning:

> Geo's new book of poems, the Carmina Catulli — O'Donnells wants to base his biography on that. Jimmy tries to explain it's a novel in verse, and

---

[77] Delany, "Sturgeon," in *Starboard Wine*, 48. Delany is here discussing Polish SF writer Stanislaw Lem's misreading of the public reception of one of American SF writer Theodore Sturgeon's short stories.

> though the characters were real, they have little to do with the period of his life they were written in.
>
> Mark Hetland was a bad poet and a pest. Not his best friend.
>
> Niva he hadn't seen in two years.
>
> Claudia, from her ideas on Women & life was probably his wife.
>
> O'Donnells relegates this to "one opinion" in the actual biography. Hardly mentions his wife at all, other than to imply that Geo was consistently unfaithful to her — very hero, very adventurous.
>
> "We're changing the facts to write a glorious biography."
>
> […]
>
> O'Donnells — "If he wasn't married, we could play up his bisexuality, but with a wife, we want to keep it down. It wouldn't look good."[78]

So grinds the mill of myth. Or — to use a critical rhetoric still inchoate in the US at the time of the novel's writing — so functions the discourse of heterosexism. Almost thirty years later, Delany would characterize this discourse as a "disarticulation that muffles and muddles all, that drags all into and within it, that represses and suppresses and lies and distorts

---

[78] Delany, *Silence*, 196. According to Delany, in the novel the Carmina Catulli was a series of poems presenting a modern re-telling of the life of Catullus, using Geo's own friends as characters (Delany, personal communication with James, March 24, 2018).

and rereads and rewrites any and every rhetorical moment within its field."[79]

One way to reinforce such distortions, of course, is to hypostatize and reify identity categories like "Woman," "Negro," "Artist," and "Homosexual," to posit them as substantive and unchanging givens.[80] And at least from *Dhalgren* on, Delany has contested this way of construing identity, positing in its stead a vision of the subject as a constant process of social making and unmaking, an "endlessly iterated (thus always changing) situation."[81] In the *Callaloo* interview, in the midst of a discussion of identity politics, Delany mentions the major categories *Voyage, Orestes!* examines and one more besides:

> All identities [...] only become interesting when they start to "leak." And the leaking process causes them to slide against and seal with others, from which they can never get free:
>
> Black with white, white with black...
> Gay with straight, straight with gay...
> Male with female, female with male...
> Mad with sane, sane with mad...

---

[79] Delany, "Street Talk / Straight Talk," in *Shorter Views*, 56.

[80] In the *Callaloo* interview, Delany recalls his "friends and contemporaries ... breaking into libraries through the summer of 1968 and taking down the signs saying Negro Literature and replacing them with signs saying "black literature" — the small "b" on "black" is a *very* significant letter, an attempt to ironize and de-transcedentalize the whole concept of race, to render it provisional and contingent" (30-31).

[81] Delany, "Coming / Out," in *Shorter Views*, 97.

> — just for the easiest (and, still, the most unsettling) of openers; and progressing at least as far as artist and non-artist.[82]

Does *Voyage, Orestes!* point the way toward this leaky identity, this internally differing, diachronic, endlessly iterated subject?

Perhaps the very unanswerability of this final question in any complete sense — due to the loss of the remainder of the manuscript — itself suggests an answer, by a kind of negative inference. The fate of the manuscript, coupled with what we find in the remaining fragment and notes, suggests that one aspect of the arithmetic of the world that the novel appears to have examined accurately, cogently, is the very mechanism of the "jinx" that would lead to its own destruction. In the name of that housewife in Nebraska — a particular instantiation of the x-variable position "woman" (indeed, "straight white woman"), an illusory center, a convenient myth, a fiction of identity — *Voyage, Orestes!* remained unpublished, unreproduced, its existence precarious, until it was too late. Whatever else the novel might have had to say beyond these opening chapters — about gender, sexuality, race, art, cities — cannot now be known. Perhaps more to the point, even before the manuscript was lost the mythic mechanism ensured that *Voyage, Orestes!* remained out of play over the whole course of the '60s, the cultural and social upheavals of which the novel, with its interplay of sex and race, myth and music, its focus on youth, and even its portentous completion the day

---

[82] Delany, "An Interview with Samuel R. Delany," 38.

before the assassination of Kennedy, was in hindsight clearly a herald, and during which it could have served as a prism, mirror, and lens. For all of Delany's efforts to shape what was about to erupt into public language at the time into a beautiful song, the jinx, call it patriarchy, made sure that that song was not heard.

It was not until the end of the decade that Delany would again attempt to tackle similar material in the context of a contemporary urban landscape: the imaginary Midwestern city of Bellona in *Dhalgren*, that extraordinary novel in which, to mix formulations from T. S. Eliot and Jorge Luis Borges, realistic fire and science fictional algebra are one.[83] And, in what I feel is a very important and still not fully appreciated moment in American literary history, *that* novel — with its laser-like focus on people of color, queer people, people inhabiting the urban underclass, marginalized people of many sorts — sold in huge numbers, and remains Delany's most widely read work.[84] Delany describes his experience of the general reader response to the novel thus:

> …the vast majority of fan letters the book received — many more, by a factor of ten, than any other of my books have ever gotten — were almost all in terms of "…This book is about my friends." "This book is about people I know." "This book is about the world I live

---

[83] Delany, "On *Dark Reflections and Other Matters*," interview by Carl Freedman, in *Conversations with Samuel R. Delany*, 192.

[84] Delany, "The Semiology of Silence," 35-37.

> in." "This book is about people nobody else writes of..."[85]

This response to *Dhalgren* was and is important because it signals the existence of an American reading audience, of an America, wildly divergent from the myths America constructs about itself. *Voyage, Orestes!* can be read, then, as Delany's first attempt to dramatize and examine, using the tools of literary realism, a truth: that these myths — of the housewife in Nebraska, the solitary homosexual, or any number of other figures in America's hallucinated pantheon — conceal wonders.

---

[85] Delany, "The Semiology of Silence," 36.

Bibliography

Bechdel, Alison. "Testy." *Alison Bechdel* (blog). November 8, 2013. http://dykestowatchoutfor.com/testy.

Biondi, Martha. *To Stand and Fight: The Struggle for Postwar Civil Rights in New York City*. Cambridge, MA: Harvard University Press, 2003.

Delany, Samuel R. "About 5,750 Words." *The Jewel-Hinged Jaw*. 1978. Revised edition. Middletown, CT: Wesleyan University Press, 2009.

—. *The American Shore*. 1978. Reprint. Middletown, CT: Wesleyan University Press, 2014.

—. "An Interview with Samuel R. Delany." Interview by Charles Rowell. *Conversations with Samuel R. Delany*. Edited by Carl Freedman. Jackson: University Press of Mississippi, 2009.

—. "Atlantis Rose…" *Longer Views*. Middletown, CT: Wesleyan University Press, 1996.

—. "Coming / Out." *Shorter Views*. Middletown, CT: Wesleyan University Press, 1999.

—. Contribution to "Forum: Writing and Politics." *Fiction International* 15:1, 1984.

—. *Dhalgren*.1975. Reprint. New York: Vintage Books, 1996.

—. "*Dichtung und* Science Fiction." *Starboard Wine*. 1984. Revised edition. Middletown, CT: Wesleyan University Press, 2012.

—. "Disch." *Starboard Wine*. Pleasantville, NY: Dragon Press, 1984.

—. Delany, *Empire Star*. 1966. Reprint. New York: Vintage Books, 2001.

—. *The Fall of the Towers*. 1966. Reprint. New York: Bantam, 2004.

—. "The 'Gay Writer'/ 'Gay Writing'…?" *Shorter Views*. Middletown, CT: Wesleyan University Press, 1999.

—. *Heavenly Breakfast: An Essay on the Winter of Love*. 1979. Reprint. Flint, Michigan: Bamberger Books, 1997.

—. *In Search of Silence*. Edited by Kenneth R. James. Middletown, CT: Wesleyan University Press, 2017.

—. "Letter to the Symposium on 'Women in Science Fiction,' Under the Control, for Some Deeply Suspect Reason, of One Jeff Smith." *The Jewel-Hinged Jaw*. 1978. Revised edition. Middletown, CT: Wesleyan University Press, 2009.

—. *The Motion of Light in Water*. Minneapolis: University of Minnesota Press, 2004.

—. "The Necessity of Tomorrows." *Starboard Wine*. 1984. Revised edition. Middletown, CT: Wesleyan University Press, 2012.

—. "On *Dark* Reflections and Other Matters." Interview by Carl Freedman. *Conversations with Samuel R. Delany*. Edited by Carl Freedman. Jackson: University Press of Mississippi, 2009.

—. "Pornography and Censorship." *Shorter Views*. Middletown, CT: Wesleyan University Press, 1999.

—. "Ruins / Foundations." *The Straits of Messina*. Seattle: Serconia Press, 1989.

— (as K. Leslie Steiner). "Samuel R. Delany." *Pseudopodium*. Ray Davis. https://www.pseudopodium.org/repress/KLeslieSteiner-SamuelRDelany.html

—. "Science Fiction and Literature — or, the Conscience of the King." *Starboard Wine*. 1984. Revised edition. Middletown, CT: Wesleyan University Press, 2012.

—. "The Semiology of Silence." Interview by Sinda Gregory and Larry McCaffery. *Silent Interviews*. Middletown, CT: Wesleyan University Press, 1994.

—. "Some Presumptuous Approaches to Science Fiction." *Starboard Wine*. 1984. Revised edition. Middletown, CT: Wesleyan University Press, 2012.

—. "Street Talk / Straight Talk." *Shorter Views*. Middletown, CT: Wesleyan University Press, 1999.

—. "Sturgeon." *Starboard Wine*. 1984. Revised edition. Middletown, CT: Wesleyan University Press, 2012.

—. "Three, Two, One, Contact: Times Square Red." *Times Square Red, Times Square Blue*. New York: New York University Press, 1999.

—. *Voyage, Orestes!*. Typescript. Delany collection, Beinecke Rare Book & Manuscript Library, Yale University.

—. "The Wiggle Room of Theory: An Interview with Samuel R. Delany." Interview by Josh Lukin. *Conversations with Samuel R. Delany*. Edited by Carl Freedman. Jackson: University Press of Mississippi, 2009.

Freedman, Carl, ed. *Conversations with Samuel R. Delany*. Jackson: University Press of Mississippi, 2009.

Mitchel, Duncan. "The Rule." *This Is So Gay*. http://thisislikesogay.blogspot.com/2009/10/rule.html.

Peplow, Michael W. and Robert S. Bravard. *Samuel R. Delany: A Primary and Secondary Bibliography*. Boston: G. K. Hall & Co., 1980.

Rimbaud, Arthur. *Arthur Rimbaud: Complete Works*. Translated by Paul Schmidt. New York: HarperCollins Publishers, 2000.

Sallis, James. Introduction to *Ash of Stars: On the Writing of Samuel R. Delany*. Edited by James Sallis. Jackson: University Press of Mississippi, 1996.

Whitman, Walt. "Song of Myself." 1881. *Leaves of Grass and Other Writings: A Norton Critical Edition*. Edited by Michael Moon. New York: W. W. Norton & Company, 2002.

GROVE PRESS, INC.
64 UNIVERSITY PLACE
NEW YORK 3, NEW YORK
OREGON 4-7200

December 20, 1963

Mr. Bernard K. Kay
220 West 42nd Street
New York 36, N. Y.

Dear Mr. Kay:

Many thanks for getting the Delany manuscript* to me. I will certainly give it very careful attention. As I told you on the phone, I think Delany has great talent.

We will come up with a specific idea by the middle of January. I'm leaving New York on Monday for a two week trip, and will return on the 6th. I'll be in touch with you within a few days after that.

Three of us have already read the first book, and one of our editors will read the long book** before I get back to New York.

Cordially yours,

BR: js

Barney Rosset

*<u>Those Spared by Fire</u>

**<u>Voyage, Orestes!</u>

Voyage, Orestes!

by Samuel R. Delany

Then voyage, Orestes, till
thou canst come home.

Prologue

1.

I have been up to Maine; and then, come down.

Scenes compress to single details: dull leaves among the forest's shadows shiver suddenly and go silver with a breeze; a black rock beside a rain-washed road harbors a dark pool of oil on water; the shattered prism of a dragonfly's wing shafted from its thin black body against a bending fern near the bottom of a waterfall —

In Vermont I came down along a grass path wide as a tractor makes, with fields of chest-high goldenrod on either side, into Massachusetts and down to the sea. The path sloped to a pine wood, and each time I put my foot down on the mat of yellowing grass, a dozen or twenty locusts sprang up about my calves like flipped pieces of gray bark. Yet all that meadow is caught for me in one clutter of sand-sized yellow granules, shivering at the end of a green stem of goldenrod — amid sextillions of others.

2.

Finding her rimmed with froth, a green glass shield below me, I started the steep trail that led from the granite embankment. The bushes grew close, and leaves lipped my cheek and shoulder. The pebbles shattered across the dirt and over rocks as I came down, and the water shone only five times through the foliage, once I started.

[Note: At this point, approximately 35 pages are missing from the "Prologue," which deal with three young people in a seaside town: Josh, Manny, and a nameless, young local woman. ("Her," is of course, the Atlantic.) At the Prologues's end, the narrator, Jimmy Calvin — whom we now know is a light-skinned black adolescent — is ready to return to his home in New York City.]

PART ONE

I. The Road

[Note: The first sixty-six type-script pages, comprising the first eight-and-a-half sections of the opening chapter, "The Road," are missing. Briefly, as does the rest of the chapter, they intercut scenes that describe the narrator's movement back to New York City with the events that led up to his leaving it. They tell of his friendship with a young writer named Geo Keller, and end with Jimmy, Geo, and some of their friends have gone to the Cloisters, the medieval museum in upper Manhattan. A young man named Paul Bherens leaves them to wander around the museum by himself. A tall young woman with a limp begins to improvise a fantastic monologue about one of the Unicorn Tapestries for which the museum is known — the incomplete, fragmentary panel. (See: "Tapestry" [under the title "The Unicorn Tapestry"], in *New American Review 9*, April 1970, Copyright 1970 by New American Library, New York, 1970. Separately this fantasia is to be found in *Aye, and Gomorrah*, pages 280-284.) It is interrupted when one of the young people, Paul, bursts through the door in one of the galleries, where he has apparently been harassing a young woman in the museum to the surprise and confusion of the other young people. They leave the museum and . . .]

offering the information. And when, that evening, we did see Paul on the subway platform where we were all waiting for the train to go down to the Village (the girl had gone home), Paul ran up to us and began to talk about some statuary that he had seen in the Cloisters on his sole wanderings, and dismissed the girl by, "God, she was crazy, wasn't she." Our vague, unspecified feelings of censure were speared and withered on the arrow points from his fasces of specific details about Gothic figures, medieval rituals, and the significance of saints, rats, and demons.

We drifted down that night through the gut of the City into the nest of lights that was the Village. Tourists, characters, green woolen sweaters, black silk blouses, all this moved by the yellow windows of coffee houses, under orange bulbs on the street lamps or in the red fire from the tail lights of gleaming cars. The streets are dirty, the fountain off at night: the great concrete circle is dry and dark, and the trees shimmer under the floods from mercury illumination. People moved through a net of muted colors under a night which draped between the buildings, smoky, and rouged with haze from the traffic lights.

The great fountain in Washington Square and the Cloisters, I have found since, are both focuses for a certain group of people in this City, or the ends of an axis about which they mentally revolve, acting as a spindle collecting all things romantic.

Now we walked through the Village streets, Karry, his shoes still over his shoulder and the soles of his feet lifting as he walked in front of me, with the pavement's filth dried into a black mud by gutter water. Niva yawned, walking slowly apart from us, and Paul and Geo walked in almost imitative rhythm side by side to my left. Martha's shortening and lengthening shadow flung out before us, dwarfed with the encroach of the streetlight, and then lengthened, again across the street, stretching and contracting through the crowds of people. I remember because she was laughing too. The night was warm, and good, and filled us with windy lamp-lit dark. And I? How was I identified, fixed to that evening; because I was. I suggested that we go to the river, and at my suggestion, made by a little boy in a red shirt, who scratched his ears, had black hair, we walked to the edge of the City, where the river spread huge and dark, like a sheet of wet rubber, across to the lights of the Navy Yard, and the smoking haze above the miniature, isolate fires that flecked the far shore. And I stood there with the others, leaning on the black gate, remembering what Martha had said, "That without the sea, or the order of rivers there is no . . ." Was it dignity? Austerity? I didn't remember[160]. But the rippling nightwater lapped at the stones; and further down, above the scattered necklaces of light, the black band of the Manhattan Bridge went darkly across the hazed midnight; the lights along with it, seemingly without order because of the angle from which we stood, make it into a belt of gems, a band of disordered beads across the river, a constellation of dragons rimming the sky.

---

[160] Martha was the name of the character in The Bridge, who, as they had wandered around the Cloisters, had improvised the monologue that became "The Unicorn Tapastry" (see *Aye, and Gomorrah . . .*)

9.

And I am sitting in a car, driving down the Thruway from Treecave[161] Massachusetts to New York, my knapsack shaking against my leg, a pale blond man driving, the sun vibrating on my lap, and in the shaking haze of light, I try to play with puppets, only to have them play with me.

A toll bridge grows in the windshield. The car slows and the man says, "You pay this toll now."

I dig down beneath the knapsack cover. The hard canvas is warm. I scrounge out the toll in silver change, hand it to him and he, in turn, hands it to the policeman in the booth as we pass. The booth is gone. The Pattern of reason and lack of reason, the past, keeps resolving itself into the present with an ending trip, a gone day in the Cloisters, or a toll booth shrinking in a rear-view mirror above a car windshield.

I sat with my hands close-cupped in my lap, in the sunlight, making shadows on the green denim, worn the whole summer. On the rim of my fingers the sun was warm. Into this cup, I tried to compress the histories of all these people.

Niva? What happened to her in the five years that separated now and then? I don't know. I can't even remember what school she went to after she graduated. I haven't seen her.

A fact that keeps exploding like a little jewel in my skull and quivering there is the realization that I am suddenly old enough to think of things in years, of people known, and people forgotten. Paul had disappeared too. When did I see him

---

[161] A stand-in for Woodshole, MA. Woodshole is the port for the ferry to Martha's Vineyard, Nantucket, and Elizabeth Islands.

last? Two years ago? Three? I don't remember how or where, other than that he grinned at me for some reason.

Karry, as always, departed with his legend trailing behind him. I got the story from Geo, who was a year behind him in school: The summer of his senior year he left home, traveled across the country, got engaged to a prostitute in a neighboring jail cell in Cheyenne, got ptomaine poisoning in the same jail, got out again, and kept on. His parents, with whom he had had a huge fight, destroyed all his manuscripts, burned his clothing, his letters, and the few volumes of journal he had not taken with him, and then sent the police out after him. "Karry's parents," said Geo, "have an unbelievable romantic fear of anything that is not completely bourgeois, to the point of attacking it in fantastically dramatic ways that would really do honor to people far more intelligent than they seemed to me the couple of times I met them." Geo had also said that Karry had given up writing and had become a very active Socialist. Having previously seen Karry, through Catholicism, Buddhism, several brands of mysticism, and yoga, I made what I thought was a witty comment about adding literature and politics to his bag of past deeds. "No," he said. "No. Karry had great talent in writing, not in those others. Great talent is great knowledge of one particular medium. Great knowledge of one medium implies respect for those who have knowledge of other media, and for the media themselves." His voice became heavy and slow, like someone working through a syllogism. "This is why a *genius* in one field is usually *talented* in many, regardless of what we say today of specialization. Remember Karry when he was writing. Talent, like wisdom, is usually more potential than kinetic. Sometimes it's mirrored by a few moments of brilliant conversation or criticism; more rarely in a brilliant work. Karry was the only person I knew with talent to frighten me. He could urge a group of words into a sentence that would snap off the page and quiver like a living thing."

Both Martha and Geo went to City College. Martha I managed to see only once in three years, a grotesquerie limping by me on the street, who either did not see or recognize me, and slumped on after I turned to watch her, further and further down the hill of Amsterdam Avenue into blue twilight. I watched her for almost four blocks. Then, though it was still not dark, the night lights flared on all up and down the street and she was lost in the bright crystal concatenation of street lamps and sweep of red, regressing tail-lights, blocks away.

Geo's departure was as silent and final as his presence had been ebullient. Two years for me filled with a hundred other people, incidents, pleasant and un-pleasant happenings. The beginning of the third year of the five between then and now, he published a book of poems. I was in my senior year, then, and the school suddenly congealed around the broken crystals of old stories. The book sold well, sold out. It was reprinted, reviewed by three critics — two who tried to out-do themselves with praise, and a third scathing enough to make the *Endymion* reviewer look complimentary. It was decided that one poem in the book, which described, among other things, a vivid castration, was obscene. Talk of a lawsuit which never materialized made a small dent in a few big newspapers, and a large dent in a couple of small literary magazines. The book sold more. It was reprinted.

And Geo was suddenly "one of the country's youngest writers, an amazing talent for one so young, an example of the terrifyingly incisive vision of youth;" and one more which seemed a little more serious than all the rest, perhaps because it was directed at the poems rather than the poet: "These poems could not have been written by a boy of nineteen."

One of the poems, in the back of the book, along with two other translations, was the Brecht poem, "*Water-Logue,*" *Vom Ertrunkenen Mädchen,* beginning:

"When she was drowned, her body was washed down
Among the streams and rivers. The pulsing
White sun gleams in the sky. (Why? To appease
Her corpse.) Winding weeds lopped and bound her,
Algae clung to her; under her feet
Dim fishes still flick silver, meet, and swim around. . . ."[162]

10.

In the cupped bowl of sun-light in my hands, histories compressed, swirled, and melted into the vibrant haze of yellow falling through the windshield. I leaned back on the seat and watched the road expanding toward us, monotonous and bright.

---

[162] Contained in Bertolt Brecht's collection *Die Hauspostille* (*Manual of Piety* [1927]). Delany previously translated the entire poem as by Geo Keller in an earlier scene in the missing sections of "The Road" in the home of a German woman in Vermont. See also *In Search of Silence*, *The Journals of Samuel R. Delany*, *Volume 1, 1957-1969*, page 105 ("Water-Logue" after [*Vom Ertrunkenen Mädchen* by Bertolt Brecht]).

I must have fallen asleep, because suddenly the car was stopping at a turn-off.

"O.K. friend," the man said, jouncing back in his seat with the declaration. "This is you."

"Thanks," I said. The knapsack was again a weight on my arm. The door was opening, and the stiffness of four hours driving was suddenly pounding from my legs. The car moved forward, sped, and was gone. I breathed deeply, twice, hoisted the bundle over my shoulder; and with the canvas sack bouncing into the small of my back, I started along the gravel siding.

I looked along the gray strip, right, left, then I ducked across the road, scrambled down the edge and started to the feed-on, fifty feet through hot, waist-deep weeds. The fields where I crossed must have been a junk heap once: between the stalks the ground was covered with rusty shale, bent brown beer cans, glass and screws, and broken parts of cars. I came to the edge of the feed-on road and sent a foot-full of cans onto the pavement with my sneaker's kick. On my jean-leg, in creases, sand had dried where it had been rolled up before. I brushed it with my free hand, and then held my open palm up. The skin had caught a scattering of grains, tiny fragments of limestone and quartz. I looked up now, across trees, over houses that sat like thrown red and green boxes in a valley a field beyond the road. And there were hills. The sea was far away.

My next hitch was with a woman in a station wagon.

"New York?" I said.

"Manhattan," the woman said. "Way uptown though."

"Fine," I said.

"Are you coming back from summer school?" she asked, as I climbed in. "What's your name? I'm Joan Firefield."

"Jimmy," I said. "Jimmy Calvin. No, ma'am. I've just been around New England for the summer."

"Staying with relatives?" the woman asked. We started.

"No," I said. "Just traveling."

"Oh," the woman said.

After a while she didn't say anything anymore, and I sat back again. She told me to put the sack in the back seat, which I did; and then there was no weight against my leg on the car floor anymore, and the trees snapped by like gems on a hypnotist's wheel.

Sitting there, I tried not to think about home; the attempt suddenly made its encroachment sting like flung sand. Thoughts of home were not refined by years but still rough and unfinished with the immediacy of weeks. It was two months ago, no, a little longer than that.

I had been walking that day along Riverside Park, quietly by brown tree trunks, slicked with sun-light, where leaves were little and quivering green. I walked along the high edge, watching the brilliant, sharp foliage beyond the low iron gate. The river was wrinkled with light, flooded with ripplings before the dimmed edge of New Jersey, evened by Spring haze. Pigeons began to fly before me; they circled low over my head and I stood there, looking at the flickering white undersides of their wings.

"Hey," someone said.

"Hello," I answered, turning around.

"Well, what have you been doing, Little Brother?"

I stared at him, trying to find changes that I could put my hands against and rub away. I may have been about to reach out and touch him, but he said, as though he had expected to meet me:

"Come with me. I want to talk to you." He put his hand on my shoulder and we were walking, without effort, down past the Church, between the trees, and along the pavement of Broadway. "How's your sister?" he asked.

"Fine," I said.

"And your mother? Is she still trying to make you pick up your room?"

"O.K."

"And your father."

"No," I said.

"No what? What do you mean?"

"He's sick," I said. I put my hands in my pockets. "He's sick."

Geo was quiet for a few steps, then he asked again. "What's wrong?"

"I don't know," I said. "He's sick."

We walked a little further.

"He had an operation," I said.

"What sort of operation?" asked Geo.

"They took out a lung," I said. "They thought it might be cancerous."

"Was it?" asked Geo.

I shrugged. "It was just an exploratory operation, and they didn't tell him that the lung was out. I found out from my cousin this morning. She's been with my mother most of the time."

"Why didn't they tell him?"

"He didn't want to know. He said not to tell him the results of the operation. I'm not supposed to know; neither is Margaret. But everybody seems to know except him."

"Well you said they didn't know if it was cancerous or not."

"Nobody knows that," I said. Then I looked at Geo. "I think they got it early. I mean, the thing they saw in the first X-rays wasn't really bad. There wasn't any pain. There wasn't any pain at all."

"All right," said Geo quietly. My face felt funny and I reached up and rubbed my mouth. Then I put my hand over my ear and rubbed that hard too. Geo put his hand on my shoulder, (we had stopped walking,) and said, "It's all right," again.

"They took out a lung," I said. "They won't tell him they took it out; he doesn't want them to tell him what they did."

"How do you know?"

"He told my mother before the operation not to tell him."

We walked on, shadows slipping under our shoes which swung out mechanically before us, slapping stone.

"They cut out his lung," I said.

"Why don't you and I sit down some place for a little while. I wanted to talk to you about a poem I've been working on. But I want to hear about you, everything that's been happening. Come on, let's go in here."

As we passed into the shadow of a candy store, a table top's Formica surface slid beneath my lowered eyes as we slipped into a booth. I looked up at Geo.

"What is your father like now?" he asked, leaning forward on his folded arms. "Your mother?"

"I donno," I answered.

"What's your father been doing?'

"Nothing," I said. "He's home, and in bed. He's very weak, and he just looks at people most of the time. He can't sleep and isn't strong enough to read the paper even. He's going to have to start exercising soon, but I don't think he'll be able to. He just stares."

"What about before the operation?"

"He was . . . I donno. He kept on telling me to obey my mother, do what she wanted; that's all he kept saying, as though he thought he was going to die then. That was all it was; take care of your mother, do what she says. Be good to her, be helpful. You couldn't get him to say a thing about himself, how he felt, what he was thinking about. He wasn't thinking; it just came out, obey your mother, like records playing over and over."

"I guess he was frightened," Geo said. "I guess he still is. What about your mother?"

"She stays with him," I said. "She sits like stone by the bed all day. Judith, my cousin, she keeps all the rest of the family informed, or not informed, and everybody else walks around and doesn't know anything. We're not supposed to let mother know we know. Mother isn't supposed to let Dad know. Nobody knows a Goddamn thing. A God damn thing . . ."

"What did she feel about the operation before it happened? Do you know?"

"I guess she wanted it," I said. "But she was scared then, only it didn't show very much. Only when we were going to the hospital to see him the night before the operation."

"Did she cry?"

"No. She sat very still all the way there in the bus. And I didn't say anything, anything at all. That's the only way I know. She sent us to see him every night — he was in the hospital three days — but she only went that once. Now she's with him all the time. He's stiff, and she rubs him with cocoa butter, and it makes the room smell like rancid grease and formaldehyde."

"Your father is an undertaker, isn't he?" Geo asked.

"Um-hum," I said.

"He sounds like someone in love with death."

I must have done something, or maybe I only shivered. Geo reached and touched my hand, and his face turned, either in upon itself, or out toward me with lines that suddenly defined its gauntness, deepened it, so that I suddenly saw him, for the first time, looking at me.

"Let's talk about you," I said.

We turned like jewels in a clock, registering time. We did talk more about my family; not about his at all. He was working on a new long poem, *The Fall of the Towers.* Two parts were finished and he wanted me to see them. "You know where I got the title from?" said Geo.

"Where?" I said.

"You remember Karry? Well, just before he started on his cross country rampage, he had begun a series of drawings with that title, or at least he'd gotten ten or twelve studies for them finished. Each panel showed a group of people, different types, reacting to something catastrophic which wasn't shown in any of the pictures. It was to have the title *The Fall of the Towers.* When his parents burned his manuscripts and drawings, though, all the work was destroyed. So, I thought maybe I could at least salvage the title."

We talked more. "How does it feel to be famous?"

"I've got a little ways to go before you'd call it famous. And I'm not making any money on it, either." He went on. Would we keep in contact? Do you live at the same place you did before?

Sure!

Then we'll drop over, or why don't you come down to see us . . . ?

"We — us who?" I asked.

"My wife and I . . . ?" said Geo. "Oh, you don't know. I've been married over a year, now."

"Huh? How old are you?" I asked.

"I was twenty-one two weeks ago."

Amazement and time ground against each other like sheets of emery cloth. Night came with more conversation and tied tight knots around us, holding us to the streets where we walked now, under cool lights, ambling, exploring again, on past mid-night.

I walked in the door, that night, just before one. Judith, in her bathrobe, was coming up the hall. When she saw me, she stopped and hissed: "For God's sake, where have you been all night! You're killing your mother with worry! You know your father isn't well, and I'd think you'd have some consideration for him."

I took two breaths and tried to say softly, but probably didn't succeed: "How's Dad feeling?"

"A lot you seem to care," said Judith, and went past and turned toward her's and my sister's bedroom. There was a noise, sheets and slow footsteps, from my parents' room. At the sound, Judith turned on me again and whispered: "Get back. You don't want him to see you like that!"

"Like what?" I said.

"Running all around the city half the night, like you've got no home to come to. Take your jacket off, anyway, for God's sake!"

She came toward me, and would have pushed me out of the hall if the door hadn't opened to my parents' room. My mother came first, and half from the room, she saw me and motioned me away. I stepped back, but couldn't go.

"Is that Jimmy," my father's voice articulated, slowly and tonelessly like tearing cloth.

My mother was supporting him, and his pajamas and robe swayed in a crush of wrinkles that covered everything but head and hands. My father wasn't looking at me, but my mother's eyes caught me, as she looked around the hall, suddenly, like flames on balsa. She raised her hands and waved me away again.

"Is that Jimmy," my father asked once more standing in the hall now where he could have seen me if he had only turned his head. "What's he doing up this late."

Then the double lung of breath broke in my throat. "Dad!" I said. "Dad, I want to tell you something. . . ." I walked forward, and my mother suddenly screamed terror at me with silent eyes and lips like a line of thread pulled across her face.

"Go away," she said, hoarsely, "and leave your father alone, now," and something like hate or disgust welled into her features, hate that I should encroach upon their doubled journey. When I saw it, I stared with the bewilderment of shattered statuary, my face beginning to shiver and fall apart like exploded stone. Where the idea flung up from, I do not know, but I suddenly said:

"Mother, Dad, I want to tell you. I'm leaving for a little while. I'm going away. I mean . . ." and the redrawn breath broke again,". . . look, I can't take it. I'm just going away for a little while. Mother?"

But she had stepped away from my father, now, and was standing with one hand on the wall, all the contortions in her face like patterns around me. "You go to your room and go to bed," she said, evenly. "Your father is sick, and you can't talk to him now."

"I'm going away," I said, and it was a whisper that shivered the roof of my mouth. "I just wanted to tell you."

The hand she held on the wall suddenly flung itself toward my face, and I jumped backward. She staggered a step forward with the missed energy. "You go to your room," she said. "You go to your room now."

I looked from my mother to my father, and then back again. My father still stood in the middle of the floor, swaying now, and looking down. A stain like a shadow descended the front of his pajama pants now, and I realized she had been taking him to the bathroom.

My mother tried to slap me again, but I whirled around, and had to grab my sister's shoulders to keep from knocking her down. Margaret had come out of her room, behind me, at the noise, and now her hands flew up in front of her face and she turned her head aside, all the world as though she thought I were going to hit her.

I pushed her away, ran down the hall to my room, flung the door closed behind me, and jerked two steps forward with the explosion of the slam. My legs were shaking and my stomach hurt, so I went down on my knees. Then I crossed my arms in front of my face, and bent down till I was resting on the floor, my body locked in the dry silent pain of gasped breaths, which flew into my mouth, again, and again, as though there were no more air.

Judith knocked on the door once, and said, "I want to talk to you. I want to talk to you about this." She waited a few minutes, and then she started again, "You're too big a boy to . . ." but then she stopped. I think she went away.

I had already begun to take things out to pack them, my mind mechanically sorting out the bits of information I would need for the journey, from camping trips, from remembered scouting handbooks, from the clutter of useless information that you store constantly from reading, conversation, and desultory experience.

I had just gotten my sister's old knapsack that she used for camp down from the top closet shelf where all our unused junk was stored when my sister came into the room. She was in her pajamas and bathrobe and she just came a step into the room and looked at me. "That's my knapsack," she said.

I flung it onto the bed with the rest of the junk I had gathered and turned back to the closet.

Then my sister said, "I'll help you pack."

It took us half an hour. When we finished, Margaret suddenly said, "You write me!" with a vicious urgency that stopped me. Then she left.

I wrote her a letter that night:

Dear Margaret,

Please try and explain to Mom and Dad. I can't. It's only because you seem to understand that I'm asking you to. I'll be back, probably near the end of the summer. I have some money, so don't worry. Not that you will. I guess this is a hell of a thing. I wish you would be with me. All very suddenly, because I never have before. I love you and I love Dad and I love Mom.

Tell them if you can,

Jimmy

I also wrote Geo:

Friend Geo,

Have to put off seeing you and your wife till the end of the summer. I'm going traveling. Home is too much. I'm glad I found you today; maybe thinking about "old times" had something to do with my decision to go. Home is unbearable because, I guess, it's a culmination of old times (home kind) gone stale, and I've gone off to look for some new old times, that'll still be fresh. Live well, I'll see you,

Little Brother.

My knapsack was heavy with little sleep the next dawn. I walked up Broadway that morning under a five o'clock sky of bleaching beryl.

I had had no sleep, and my stomach was filled with a knot of unrealized fatigue. Cars were going by, and the sky and the pavement both seemed equally far away. My wallet made a square of my buttocks sweat; my knapsack straps burned my shoulders, but I walked. When I began seeing signs directing me toward the bridge, I suddenly realized how far I'd come. Another building corner drew back, and suddenly I was standing before the entrance to the bridge, a double sweep of steel over the morning water. The cars were rolling fast, the foot path entrance was ahead of me, and the sun had just vaulted the seared horizon.

Suddenly I began to run, the pavement beating up against my feet and battering me toward the sky. As I reached the bridge, the low sun scoured away the suspension cables with hot, orange light so that the main supporting cable seemed to rise free, pure curved against blue sky, and I was running, light with leaving.

11.

The car stopped, and the woman turned toward me: "Well," she said, "I guess you're just about home."

II. The Bridge

1.

I phoned them just before I arrived at the house from a booth on the corner. Clickings, ringing of phone bell, and then the jiggle of the receiver lifting.

"Hello?" my mother's voice asked with unfamiliar plaintiveness.

"Hello," I said. "Mom?"

"Jimmy?" my mother said. "Where are you?"

"Mom?" I said again. "I'm home, Mom."

"I mean where are you?" she asked again with the wavering, unfamiliar voice she used with strangers.

"I'm in a phone booth," I said. "I'll be up in a little while, as soon as I can get there."

"All right," she said.

I breathed twice. "How is everybody?" I asked.

She didn't say anything, and suddenly something exploded again and again inside my chest. I breathed. "Is Margaret O.K. too?"

"Judith went home."

"Oh," I said. The beating in my ear and jaw was so loud I could hardly hear the voice attenuated by metal coils and black plastic.

"Dad?" I said.

"What?" asked my mother.

"How's Dad?"

"He's . . . better," said my mother.

"Oh," I answered. "That's good." The explosions got almost twice as loud and then began to go down.

"You come on home," my mother said. "You come on home now."

"All right," I said. Then the phone clicked. I hung up and leaned up against the back of the booth. After a minute or so, I went out again and walked up the darkening street. Vivid blue went down behind the houses and a ribbon of bright light was fading just along the roof-tops. The evening was warm.

Doubt suddenly leapt into my throat and struck at the back of my tongue like a snake and hung there, coiling down the length of me. Mother had said that Dad was . . . better. And then the explosions started again.

I had only written two letters to Margaret since I'd left; and I had never been in a place where I could receive any. The knapsack swinging from the end of my arm was like a lead bubble.

I reached the house; I opened the front door; I started up the stairs. Just then Margaret walked around the head of the steps. She saw me, stopped, and then grinned like flowers under moonlight. She ran down the steps toward me, and at the same time calling, "Jimmy's back! Mom, Jimmy's home. Mom, *Dad,* he's back!"

She hugged me hard, and then hugged me again so that the bones of her arms and shoulder locked into my chest and back, as though strung with thin wire. Then she took one knapsack strap while I carried the other and walked upstairs.

Dad was stronger, they said. And he smiled at me. Dinner was over, but Mother fixed something in the kitchen and I ate there. They said they were glad I was home, and I kissed them all. Mother, putting food in front of me, said, "I was worried to death. I'm glad you're here. I was so worried."

And when I hugged my father, sitting in his dark room, he laughed and said, "Not too hard. I haven't got all my strength back yet."

Later my sister told me to take a bath because I stank, which I guess I did. Then, when the windows were shiny black paper, punctured by yellow lights from other windows across the street, and warm familiarity returned with the smell of linen closets opened for new sheets, the sliding rasp of chest-of-drawers runners, the unfolding of clean pajamas with old patterns I knew; then we sat in the living room and relaxed. Mom brought Dad out and she sat down in the green chair, swaddled in bathrobe and pajamas. He had to use an old zinc pail to spit into; he said his throat was bothering him. He would hawk and then there would be a metallic *thwnnng* on the pail bottom. Margaret sat on her feet in the big arm chair across the room, and then mother came in with tea for everybody. After Dad said he didn't want any, I told about the trip. I told about the mountains, and rough roots I'd used as dusty hand-holds to climb them, about farmers I'd seen standing and looking down rocky slopes and cussing quietly. I'd picked up rocks to make walls for three days, once; the farmer told me that the walls were not really important, but just to get the rocks out of the fields. But the stone lines grew higher, and wound long and gray down through the brown-green slopings. Then I spoke of the rimless sea, Josh, Manny, and the girl who had drowned, of all the ships there, and all the bright water that had lapped to me.[163]

Just then, Dad got up and began to walk slowly out of the room. He swayed so much I thought he was going to fall. Surprise kept me seated, but mother was suddenly next to him and supporting him. Together they left the room.

I looked at my sister, puzzled.

"He's just tired," she said. "I guess it's easier to just get up and go when you're like that instead of having to say anything. He's been up more today than since before the operation."

"Does he know about his lung being gone?" I asked, softly.

"Not yet," said Margaret. "But he's getting stronger."

"Oh," I said, wondering.

That night I went to sleep early, molding into the curve of pillow and mattress more like something powdered from sea salt or marble than a living thing. I slept late.

---

[163] This is a reference to the narrative referred to in Note 1 in the missing "Prologue."

2.

I found Geo's letter, along with other sundry mail I had received over the weeks, the next morning. ". . . come down and talk . . ." it said among other things. The day chilled to afternoon, and silence webbed spider strands through the house, now; having welcomed me, they could think of nothing else to do. And neither could I. So, that evening, I came down through narrow streets, packed with garbage cans, past condemned houses with shattered windows and tinned doors, until I finally found the apartment house whose address corresponded to that on the letter.

The floors of the hall were grimed-over tile and the wall had dropped scabs of paint. I walked two flights of decaying steps; the stone edges, worn down in the middle, gave the impression that the stone itself had bowed.

I found the apartment on the third story and light lined the lower edge of the door; sound came from inside, so I knocked. No one answered. I knocked again, and was going to try once more because of the light when tumblers began to thud, and then the door was tugged back from the jamb.

"Hey, Little Brother," Geo said, standing in the splay of light.

"I came down to see you and your wife," I said. "I got your letter. I just came in yesterday."

"Oh, thanks," Geo said. Then he said, "Look, Little Brother, I can't really invite you in just now. Can you sort of set a specific day and tell me when you'll be coming?"

"Oh, sure," I said. "Anytime that's O.K. with you. What's going on?"

"We are in the process of having a marital squabble," Geo said.

"Oh," I said, "I'm sorry." Embarrassed and shrinking. "No, sure, I'll come back some other time."

"Thanks, Little Brother," said Geo. And then he stepped back and the door jumped closed. I stood for a moment, listening. The sound from inside could have been crying. I turned around and started down the stairs, an unresolved disappointment quivering lightly in the mask of my face. I left the building, had just gotten half way down the block, when a splatter of footsteps struck the street behind me. "Hey, Little Brother," I heard a voice.

I turned. "How come you're here?" I asked.

"I walked out," Geo said.

"Huh?"

He took a large breath, and instead of answering, said, "Well, now let's talk about you."

I decided I was not going to be not-answered today: "What was happening up there?"

"Just an argument," Geo said.

"Who won," I asked.

"Nobody," said Geo. "I walked out. People don't win these things."

"Does this happen often?" I ventured, after a few steps.

"We have our periods," Geo said. "We have lasted together now for two years and don't see separation coming in the near future. Take that as an achievement."

"O.K.," I said. "You still haven't told me who your wife is."

"You didn't ask," Geo said. "I don't think you know her. Her name used to be Laile Lane."

Man, only the manifestations look different. My wife comes from a home of plastic couch covers and contour sheets; never been allowed to go to camp long enough to learn how to make her own bed. She's never mopped a floor, never was taught how to hold a broom. Modern Mother, in order to see that Modern Daughter was never relegated to the Position of Woman, withheld this knowledge and saw that Modern Daughter had a fine education. At the same time instructing her never to show her brains too much or she will never catch Modern Man, who will feel threatened by such a show; Modern Mother thoroughly pounds this into her head, with the help of Modern Father, that she must be on her guard against Modern Man who will disdain her on first sight, consider her inferior, and whom she must coax, deceive, and trick by every wile available; yet she must be proud that she is a Woman, and never let herself be simply used as one; in short, Modern Woman is left as a completely useless, thoroughly frustrated member of society, capable at most of being a witty parasite. My beloved wife hit marriage at a fairly young age with no household survival skills, disconcertingly discovered that her husband had them; and this ability to mop floors, make beds, and wash windows which she was always told were despicable jobs for a woman to be forced to do and really beneath human endeavor, is suddenly something that becomes imperative for a minimum of sanitation. She resents not knowing it, and she resents someone else knowing it: she takes refuge in her fine education, which includes psychology, and goes through all my previous analysis beautifully, and then, contented, sits back, assured that she has uncovered the problem, in a growing pile of soiled laundry. But the squalor depresses her too; depresses her more than it does me; I, at least, know how to do something about it when I have to. For her it is something outside her whole sphere of education. She wants to be useful, wants to get out and work. She gets a job, must prove herself; no . . . no . . . she can't fail and sink back into that horror of housework which her husband can even do (housework that she's never done, which makes her wonder why it should be so depressing to her, or maybe that's the answer). What *should* be the learning experience of a job is taken for a "test" experience to prove herself. Mistakes are made and hidden, rather than corrected, great amounts of necessary information are muddled instead of memorized, and over it all sits a mask of cool objectivity which she must maintain at any price for fear she is going to be considered inefficient. To an employer this looks like monumental unconcern, and this coupled with the secreted mistakes and the usual muddle make the ordinary amount of inefficiency from inexperience loom like waves of feminine incapability. The job is lost, she is back at the house, and the wheels clicks one circle further."

"What was your particular problem this evening?" I asked. "I still don't understand."

"I finally ordered her to make the beds. She said I couldn't give her orders. I said that until she brought home some money, or made it easier for us to survive one way or another, although I may not be able to give her orders, I could kick her out if she didn't obey them; that she was hindering my survival, and I was not hindering hers.

"Tisk, tisk," I said.

"She said I didn't understand her, and I agreed, and left, you having wrung the bell about three seconds before."

"Oh," I said. "Hey, where did you learn to do all this housework of which you are apparently so capable, anyway?"

"I was very dutifully taught by my mother so that my wife would never have a husband who couldn't help her around the house."

"Your mother seems to have been very considerate of your wife."

"Oh, no," said Geo, "this was when I was six years old. My mother is a rather Gothic woman — I think you met her once — and inculcated ideas like that with a force that still leaves me shaking today."

"Oh, now it begins to come out," I laughed. "Who feels intimidated by *whom*? You mother has imposed on you the burden of being a housewife as well as supporting your family; I don't remember your being particularly friendly to your mother. Your wife makes you live up to this, and you resent it terribly. You know, you must be unbearable to live with. You act like a cornered guinea pig; not only that, but your mother isn't around, so how is your wife going to see where one of the walls that's holding you in is. As far as she's concerned, and rightly so, be she modern human being, modern woman, or what all, you're a regular little tyrant."

"Strange," said Geo. "She said something to that effect." Then he lifted his head and laughed. "Of course you're not telling me anything I don't already know, or that she doesn't know either. It's all in the expression, in the ability to articulate the problem someway between the two of us and together rebel against it; even singly, if either of us could alone, then there would be no problem for the other. But neither of us seems to be able to commit themselves to such a display of strength."

"Won't your face be red if you come home and find the beds made," I said. "You probably wouldn't know what to do."

With a seriousness that had gone from our talking up till now, Geo said, "You know you're right."

We were descending streets smoked blue by evening. Mercury lights were on the lamp poles, bright display of luminescences imbedded in thin fog. "What about you," asked Geo. "Why did you pick this evening to come down?"

"I've been back a couple of days . . . no, one day. But I wanted to see you. How's your poem coming?"

"Which poem?"

"*The Fall of the Towers,* the one you told me about before I left."

"I haven't worked on it since a couple of days after I saw you. You remind me to take it out again. I've been turning on a few little things. They're sort of relaxing. How's your father?"

"Fine," I said. "Much better."

"Your letter made knots in all sorts of things I had almost thought I'd untangled about you," said Geo.

"How do you mean?"

"Like tying curtains together. Something happened, pretty rough that made you take off. And you still have to tell me about your trip."

"Nothing happened," I said. "I just decided to go. I guess I was just pretty upset that day. Dad is a lot healthier than I thought. He looks a lot better. He was up last night."

"I'm glad," said Geo. "But it was a funny letter. Is your sister all right?"

"She's fine," I said. "Things are really fine. You come back from a trip, and then things settle again. I don't think I should have gone, now. Oh, it was a lot of fun, and I have stories to tell you from it. But, thinking about it, I guess I was being a little cruel, my father so sick then."

"If that's the way it is," Geo said, "then I'm happy for you. But the letter you sent me made it seem a little more serious than that."

"I was upset," I said. "I was very upset. I'm all right now though."

"What about your trip, then?"

And, as we neared the circle below the base of the great bridge that leapt through the fog toward Brooklyn, I began the narration of my summer's adventure. As we talked, we wandered across the asphalt arena, siding cars, and passed beneath the bluish stone arches onto the walk that went along the bridge's edge. Steel cables dripped black against the heavy blue ship yards across the water. We went slowly, a breeze catching at our wrists and necks, and I came to the story of Josh, Manny, and the nameless woman. Having recounted it once to my family, I felt free within the story and blue wind on the bridge. As I finished telling it, we turned and leaned on the cold metal railing that lined hard under our arms, looking at the wet skin of the river, smooth and reflective, under the dim, lowering gauze of sky; and the hoop of lights around us on the closing shore, at whose center, now, we were suspended in the net of steel, above and below joined disks of blue.

"Sick kid," Geo said, a few seconds after I had finished the story.

"What do you mean?" I said, "Who?"

"Josh."

"How? Why him?"

"You're going to have to forgive me this evening," Geo said, looking still into the coming dimness around us. "I have this one thought, and everything I hear or see seems to get turned into evidence to support it? It all goes back to the argument I was having with Laile."

"What thought?" I asked.

"I told you, the inability to rebel." He shrugged his shoulders in. Late summer nights were chill out over the water. "This is just another example; although, I confess that everything is going to seem like another example of it until tomorrow morning when something else comes into my head."

"Who not rebelling against what?" I asked.

"Josh, staying in the situation. Admittedly, from what you told me, the whole town was pretty sick, but that he should stay there, be in the same boat with Manny, take you to the restaurant where the woman had fought with him on the beach was, so quietly, with such docility, though it has Christ-like attributes about it all, he seems to be guilty of the epitome of their sins. The larger horror of the whole thing is that he couldn't recognize the evil, and apparently, as of two days ago, or however long it was that you saw him, still can't recognize it. And this, this is his own violation's doing, and so links him up with the whole thing. You're getting that story, and then going away, and leaving him still sleeping peacefully in the boat, in that town, with those people: that's my wife telling me quite logically how she has been duped by parents and society into resenting housework and what all, and then sitting back and letting herself act as though she were still being duped. The understanding of it leaves them both responsible, it seems to me, for what befalls them. And the inability to move seems such a sickness! The sickness that self- destructive governments suffer from, that perhaps I suffer from in staying where I am: the understanding is there: why doesn't anyone move! Like you with your family. But then at least you did go away, even if you came back. You were in an unpleasant situation, and left."

"No," I said. "I wasn't in an unpleasant situation. I just decided to go."

"That's not what your letter said," went on Geo. "What exactly happened the night you wrote me. Something did, I've known you too long not to know that something went wrong."

"Nothing went wrong," I said. "I . . . I wasn't thinking about them, I was only being selfish, just thinking about myself. I shouldn't have gone, I told you that. I'm sorry I did now, and it's all right. Everything's fine now."

"You told them you were going to go and they yelled at you?" asked Geo, with the growing cynicism of disgust, but at what I could not opine.

"They didn't yell at me," I said. "They didn't. I was just being selfish. They came to my door to reason with me, but I wouldn't let them in. My cousin, she wanted to talk to me reasonably about it, but I shut her out."

"You went anyway, with their yelling, and now you're back and they're halfway decent to you, probably out of respect that you were able to go, and you feel guilty as hell about it and will probably do all you can to make sure they lose whatever respect they've gained."

"That's not true," I said. "It's not."

"If you have the understanding, you don't move;" said Geo. "And when you do move, and assert yourself, I look for the understanding behind it, and I find it's gone, or it never was there in the first place."

He pushed himself away from the railing and turned back toward the city.

"It's not like that," I said once more; and then in the silence of our voices, the thin sound of breeze and cars rolling past, we walked side by side back toward the shore. When we reached the shore, I said once more, and my voice seemed now somehow strained, "It's not as simple as that. Not just like that."

"I know," said Geo. "I know. But its complexities can be understood. Don't kid yourself, friend. Just don't do that." Then he said, "Look, you must come down again, sometime soon. There's all sort of people I want you to meet. You remember Paul Behrens? I've seen a lot of him, lately. He may be around. Bring your sister. I want to say hello to her too. And I hope you father gets well soon. I'm glad to hear he's better."

"Thanks," I said, glad that the subject had disappeared. "Thanks. I hope you get the squabble with Laile settled."

"Oh, we will," Geo said. "It was good to see you again."

And then I turned off toward the subway. Night lopped black down through the transparent evening, and hovered at last just above the street lights, like bolts of quivering velvet.

3.

I don't know where this comes, or why it should come now. I know my thoughts after that evening, as I sat on the subway going home, progressed, for a time nearing the half score, the same road they had taken on my way home from Massachusetts, piercing incidents an eleventh and twelfth time, leaving them shredded like rags. And the last incident was the same; my departure, my mother and father in the hall, the face of my sister as I whirled on her, sudden motions and sharp sounds, now blunted with my own guilt, and annealed by what became with retrospection, Geo's accusation. And in the flame of his disgust and my disgust, this happened:

My mother drove us to Jersey, the last warm day of the year. The day before, my father had been his best, and had assented, assuming he felt equally well the next day, to make the visit. The day was clear, and he was better, than ever before. So, by two o'clock, Margaret and I were getting out of the car in front of my Aunt Holmer's house, and then slowly walking behind Mom and Dad, past the hedge, along the cracked flag stones, and up the brick stoop. Trees veered tall above the door and sluffed leaves gently, as we came in. The sun on the lawn was brilliant.

For early dinner, there was red ham with crust seared amber, run by slashes, dotted with the black, pronged cloves, and the bone, protruding like a broken pike from a belly, charred so slightly around the edges. There were tureens of dark leafy vegetables, and one bowl of thick, hot cream sauce, in which onions floated like blunted icebergs in the polar sea. There were large glasses of punch the color of powdered carmine and water which were impossible to drink if you inhaled just before putting the glass to your mouth, because the microscopic spray of bubbles inspired would burst along your palate and the back of your tongue and pucker your mouth like new persimmons.

In all this my father sat, thrust at by many handed relatives, talked to and congratulated on his improvement, eating very little, and smiling tiredly.

Then he went to the living room, a thickly carpeted chamber in which there was a dead fire place, and fell asleep in a large, mute-red chair. A flamingo, six inches high, blown of clear scarlet and milky white glass stood on the mantel piece, doubled by the mirror, watching him.

Night smoked the windows blue, and blue fell into black. Pale boredom twisted through the house, now, like smoke, and I followed its sifting from room to room, wandering without purpose from the third floor to kitchen, from kitchen to my aunt's bedroom, and thence to the dismantled dining room where the mahogany table, still unfolded, made an arena for the chandelier's reflection, and the silver chest sat open on the sideboard, with glittering silver bones. The table cloth was folded near it, the chairs all taken out, the conversation quiet in half a dozen other rooms, and so, with light tiredness about me, I walked out on the back porch, and dowm to the dark lawn. As I reached the driveway, blue-black gravel scuttled under my feet as I went. Finally I reached the triangle of light from the street lamp, which cut a straight shadow. My father, apparently having woken and decided to take a walk, was standing down the block, just near the corner.

I started toward him, slowly. The pavement was swatched with black shadow, or cracked by great oak tree roots that pyramided it at intervals. My father turned around when I was about three feet away from him at the sound, and I stopped.

"Hey," he said, sort of smiling and looking puzzled at me.

"How you feeling," I asked.

"Tired," he said. "I thought I'd get some air, walk around the block, but the corner is as far as I can make tonight." He laughed. We stood there together on the corner. The night was cool, sharp, but still. Finally my father turned and we started back. A thought began to worm in my gut, stirring in the quiet of darkness: why not ask him now? Then, and this frightened me, my insides contracted away from it as though it were cold and slimy, and I realized there was fear in my body: "Dad," I said, the thought crawling into my tongue, "what about the operation?"

"What do you mean about it?" he asked.

I realized I'd meant to say, Dad, they took out your lung in the operation, and you're getting stronger, and everybody knows it but you, and you're really fine so it's all right. "You never told us what they found out." I know you don't know what they found, you didn't ask, you don't want to know!

"I never found out either," he said, laughing. "I don't think I really want to know."

"Doesn't Mother know?"

"Yes," he said, after a second.

"Well isn't it sort of hard on Mother, leaving it all to her; and besides, you're getting better, and they were only after something they saw on the x-rays and you weren't having any pain or anything before." And urgency pushed my voice in the dark; hearing it, I stopped. And then went on, "And don't you think you'd feel better if you knew? Then you wouldn't have to worry."

"I don't know, Jimmy," my father said.

We reached the yellow light from the porch, and entering the bright foyer, the hesitant continuation that gelled like phlegm in my throat, dissolved and flowed with coming conversation of mother, sister, and cousin, who entered the room together, speaking of departure; "There you two are. It's late; you'll be dead tired tomorrow if we don't get home soon. You've had a day."

Coats were rushed from the closet, flared and collapsed to quivering grays and browns; my sister's was bright red. Then back outside and into the car.

Receding lights sheered up my mother's face as we drove away. Mercury brilliance lined her knuckles on the wheel, and the concentrated linings on her face filled and emptied with shadow as the lights passed.

The next day, sitting by the bedroom window, my father said to me, suddenly, yet without excitement, "Well, I know."

I had come to get a book from the bedroom bookshelf. "Huh?" I asked.

"They took the damn lung out. I guess it could have been worse."

"You asked?"

"Um-hm," my father said. "Now at least I know why I've been having all this trouble breathing. I guess I'll get used to it in time, though."

"That's good," I said.

That evening the doctors told Mother over the phone that they wanted Dad to have just a few more tests. No, there was nothing to be worried about, it was just routine. Really didn't think he should be bothered with a car ride. The ambulance would come that evening. And at eight o'clock, the efficient clatter of attendants' feet rattled down the hall like flung white-ivory dice.

They impaled the apartment like bleached whale ribs through soft fruit. Straps dangled, canvas was unrolled with the snap of a descending home-movie screen, and then someone said, "Now just relax, Mr. Calvin."

And my father was on the stretcher and half strapped in.

"Excuse me," my father said, "that strap is too tight. It's hurting my leg."

"Just relax, Mr. Calvin," and fingers leaped to slack band which flew taut through a silver buckle.

"Ow!" said my father. "That's too tight!"

"Just relax, Mr. Calvin."

Buckle, twist, pull . . .

"God damn it! Get out of here!" and the jittering of white arms suddenly slacked before a far more violent heaving, rending, sound of torn canvas, and my father suddenly stood up among the astonished male nurses while quivering activity stopped now like spun white poker chips flattened on a table.

"I said get out of here!" rumbled my father. He flopped one hand on the shoulder of one of them and turned him toward the door and pushed, herding the others forward with a look and another curse that reflected each other in vigor.

"Just relax, Mr. Calvin."

They were in the hall by this time.

"Just re— "

With the snap and ring of broken steel plating, the hall doors were flung shut. My father turned now, looking from my mother, to me, to Margaret who had all gathered behind him. "They have no respect for a sick man. No respect at all."

Then, slowly, he walked back towards his room, entered, got into bed, and leaned up against the head board, breathing deeply, deeply with gulping inhalations.

Later that evening, Judith came, and together we drove Dad over to the hospital. "Yell when you're going to bump," he said. "It hurts like hell." He spoke softly, and Judith turned around to look at him.

At the hospital they had a wheelchair waiting for him in the receiving room.

"Do you need that?" Mother asked.

My father shrugged.

"Why don't you let your son take you upstairs, Mr. Calvin?" the nurse asked, smiling at me. The nurse helped him into the wheelchair, and then with her preceding, I rolled the leather and metal web along the ramp and into the yellow tiled walls of the hospital. Dad sat back, quiet, and the lines that separated the tiles made a net of the walls and floor down which we were rolling like silver fish.

"We'll take the X-rays this evening," the nurse said, "and then we can get started on the tests bright and early tomorrow morning."

We turned into a corridor which opened up into cubicles, locker alcoves, and X-ray rooms.

"Just go right in there," the nurse said. "You can help him undress," she told me. "I'll have an attendant bring you a smock."

We rolled into a cubicle the size of a closet, and I helped Dad onto the bench at the back. I could feel the bones in his hand heavy and loose in their skin when he leaned on my shoulder for support. "How do you feel?" I asked.

Dad shrugged again.

His clothing was loose, and came off like sloughed hide on a molting animal. His skin, beneath the opening shirt, clung skeletally to him like wet cloth clings to your fingers. We had to stop a lot, because he was tired and there wasn't really enough room to move around and keep clothes straight. A smock was flung over the top of the door, and when I started to put it on him, he said, "Let me just rest a minute."

He sat very still, tall, and thin, naked on the bench in the slough of clothing. After five minutes, when he had made no move to put on the smock, I raised his arm to slip it in the sleeve. "Let me just rest," he said again, but he let me put it on him.

When I opened the door, the attendant was standing beside the door, a short, once very strong man, whose edges seemed to have been blunted. His head was frizzled with yellow hair no longer than the nap of a rug. He smiled, and came in to help Dad into the wheelchair. Then we went down the corridor to the X-ray room. The rubber handles on the back of the chair were cool, even clammy.

The door was too small for the wheelchair.

"You want me to help you to the table?" the attendant asked.

The top of the X-ray table was smoothly black, hollow with the reflection of the equipment above it. The attendant took Dad by the arm, and helped him from the wheelchair and walked him over to the table. “You just sit down here and stretch out.”

Dad sat on the table. “It’s cold,” he said.

“Just stretch out,” the attendant said. “You can do it.”

“I can’t,” Dad said.

The attendant motioned me over, and I stepped around the wheelchair and came in.

“We’ll help you.”

Together we tried to lift his legs onto the table.

“Don’t let me fall” he said. His hands were holding tight to the black table edge.

“Just relax,” the attendant said. “We won’t let you fall.”

The smock kept slipping off his legs and he would try to reach down and cover them, but then his hand would snap back onto the table edge. “I’m going to fall,” he said.

“You’re all right now,” the attendant said. “Stretch your legs out. That’s right.” The attendant pushed the bent knee down. The ligaments beneath the joint pulled in the dull flesh like wires.

“You can stay with him now,” the attendant said. He adjusted the double black bulb above the table, slipped in the plate, and retired behind a wall in the room. “Stay very still, and take a deep breath, hold it . . .”

“I’m going to fall,” Dad said again. “I’m going to fall!”

“Hold it,” the attendant said. “That’s right. There we go. It’s all right now, Mr. Calvin.”

My father’s hand was wet and cold as rags.

"Roll over on your side, now," said the attendant.

"I can't," my father said.

"We'll help you," the attendant said, coming from behind the wall again. He took my father's shoulder, and tried to roll him over on his side.

The hand snapped like blown paper against the black top, and sliding across sweat marks that dried wavering almost instantly.

"Just turn to your side," the attendant said. "You're not going to fall. Your son's right here, he'll hold you."

"It's cold," my father said. "Hold me. Please, please, I'm going to fall. I'm going to fall, help me."

The attendant was adjusting the equipment, fast now. The smock slopped off my father's back and it bared up white like wet marble. "Help," he said. "I'm falling! Help me. Oh God, please help me."

"I've got you," I said. "I'm right here."

"I'm falling. Oh God, help me." He was crying now. "Help. Help. Help me!"

The attendant went back behind the wall. "That's right. Just hold on."

"I'm falling," Dad cried. "Help me."

"That's right," said the attendant. "There we go."

He came out from behind the wall again.

"Help," Dad said again, "please."

"It's all over now," said the attendant. He raised the equipment. Dad was wet all over and the tears were running down his face as we sat him up. He couldn't walk to the wheelchair so we had to carry him.

The attendant looked at me for a second. "You can leave him with me now. There's a bathroom down the hall if you want to wash your face and hands. Then you can come back and see him in his room."

The attendant took Dad's wheelchair and started down the hall. Dad sat very still and very hunched. As I turned to go, I saw another man coming from the cubicle where I had undressed him, with his clothes hanging neatly over his arm.

When I came to where mother, Judith, and Margaret were waiting, my mother got up. "Are you all right?" she asked.

"Sure," I said. "I'm fine. Just tired."

"How's your father?"

"He's all right now," I said. "You can go up to his room and see him now."

"You look very tired," she said again. "Are you going to stay?"

"I'm going home," I said.

"All right," said Mother.

They turned, now, and I watched the three women going out the door, and shrinking along the florescent brightness of the yellow hospital corridor.

4.

I walked home, up Broadway, and the daylight was high and faintly green behind a tight gauze of cloud. The open doors of bars let chittering music scuttle onto the street from rainbow juke boxes, and there was a radio in one window, singing through the continuous rustle of static.

The air was neutral and cool. The trees on the island that divided the wide way were tall, thin, shadowless beneath the filmed sky; and when I reached Julliard, the hail of bar music had faded into the stately cacophony of a hundred pianos, trumpets and cellos, all limning different lines of myriad counterpoint, each through an open window of a practice room, each practice room, in turn, sunk like an imploded bubble in the heavy, gray building.

Angles of sound, fans of piano runs spread and grew as I approached, and then diminished as I passed on. Just as I neared my corner, heavy above the last filigree of music from behind me, came the first bell boom from the carillons as the evening service began at the church. One quarter of the sky, as I stopped to listen now, had filled with blue, deeply twisted with loops of gray clouds, beautiful, ominous as waves. At home there was a letter for me.

> Dear Jimmy,
>
> We would like very much for you to come down for dinner this week. What about Friday? Geo has talked about you for a long time and I am anxious to meet you. Some of our friends will be there, and if Margaret wants to come, please bring her. Geo has told me that your father is ill but getting better. I hope everything works out well. We will be looking for you Friday evening,
>
> Sincerely,
> Laile Keller

I just finished the letter when doors opened outside, and I heard Mother, Judith, and Margaret getting back from the hospital. Coats, closet doors; I folded the letter up and put it back in the envelope.

A few minutes later, Judith half opened the door and said, "Hi. Can I come in?"

"Sure," I said. She came in and sat down on the bed. "How's Dad?" I asked.

"He finally got to sleep before your mother left. She came home to fix dinner for you and Margaret. She'll be going back to the hospital later tonight."

"Oh. I guess none of the tests have come through?"

"Oh yes," she said. Then she paused. "The other lung is malignant."

"He's going to die?"

"Yes," Judith said.

"How long?"

Judith shrugged. "Two weeks. A month. I don't know."

"Does Mother know?"

"Yes," Judith said. "Margaret doesn't yet. I think you should tell her if you feel like it. I mean I think she'd take it better coming from you. If you feel you can, I mean. He isn't in any pain or anything. They've given him something for that."

"I'll tell her," I said.

"All right," said Judith. Then she got up and went outside.

When I went into Margaret's room, she was at the desk, writing. "What do you want?" she asked.

"How are you feeling?"

"Tired," she said, looking up.

"Dad's very sick," I said.

"I know."

"He's going to die very soon."

She tilted her head a bit. "Oh." Then she went back to her letter. "We should go back to the hospital tonight with Mother."

"All right. Are you O. K.?"

"I'm fine," said Margaret.

"Oh," I said. "We have an invitation to see a friend of mine for dinner at the end of this week. Maybe we'll be able to make it."

"All right," said Margaret. "Could you leave me alone now?"

"Oh. Sure," I said. I went out of the room. Just like that. Really.

The hospital room that night was cubical crystal sheered by florescent blades. The uncles and aunts had started gathering in clusters like withering buds. Inside the room they had set up the oxygen tent over him. It shimmered with my father's breath, like transparent flies' wings. My mother stood very close to the side of the bed and held his hand through the tent. There were tubes in his nostrils. The nurse, at the other side of the bed was tucking in the blanket. He was awake, and smiled at us when we came in.

"How are you feeling?" I asked.

"Oh," he said. "So so. I can breathe much better now since. . . ." he paused. "Oxygen."

"That's good." I said.

"I wish they'd let me shave," he said.

"You can shave tomorrow," the nurse said. "After you get some sleep. You're much too tired now."

Dad smiled a little.

I moved aside to let Margaret get there.

"Hi," she said. "Are you getting fed?"

"I think so," he said. "I think that's what this is." Another tube ran under a bandage on his arm. Margaret suddenly bent over and kissed the transparent covering. "That's for you," she said. "Can you feel that?"

"I think so," he said.

"Good," said Margaret.

"I don't want him to talk too much," the nurse said. "He's very tired."

"I love you," Margaret said.

Dad smiled.

And the smile came back again on her face.

"Are you all right at home . . . ?" Dad started.

"*Shhhh* . . ." she said. "Everything's fine. I'm all ready to go back to school. Everything's fine."

"As long as you're here," the nurse said, smiling, "I'm afraid he's going to talk. You can come see him again tomorrow." She nodded us toward the door.

"Jimmy," Dad said.

"You've got to be quiet, Mr. Calvin," the nurse said.

I turned back. "Take your mother home," he said. "I'll be fine."

"We'll see that she gets home," said the nurse. "Be quiet now."

Mother stepped back up to the bed quietly. Dad lay back on the pillow and closed his eyes. He was breathing very hard, and there was a sound, even through the tent, like wind in old tissue paper. He opened his eyes and watched me again, and his face had the look of someone who has just forgotten something but is trying to recall it. The nurse nodded us again toward the door, and we turned and left.

Mother got home later. "He's resting," she said. Then she shook her head. The house dropped into night; lights went out like candles plunged in water. I sat in my room, paced, changed into old clothes, read, sat some more. At last I took a notebook, a pencil, put on my coat and walked down the hall toward the door.

"Jimmy?" my mother said. She was sitting in the living room in her bathrobe. "Where're you going?"

"Just out to walk for a little while," I said.

"Do you have to?"

"I just want to go out," I said. "I won't be long."

"Don't go away."

"Do you want to talk?" I asked. "Shall I sit with you?"

"No," she said. "No. I just want you in the house. I don't want you to go away. I think we should all be together."

"I'm not going away," I said. "Just for a little while. I'll be back in half an hour at most."

"I wish you wouldn't."

I breathed deeply twice, opened the door, and closed it quietly behind me. Outside, I took my shoes off and left them on the door mat. Then I walked along the cold hall floor, down the stairs, and out into the street.

It was raining just slightly.

The air fogged and haloed the street lights. The pavement was rough and wet under my bare feet. By the time I reached the corner, you couldn't tell if it were raining or not anymore. There were no people on the street. Store windows were backed by dead dark. The buildings leaned together above me. I was walking for the river, and the great undulance of park that sided it.

When I walked up the steps to the plaza of Grant's Tomb, my feet brushed through wet leaves, and I could see across to Jersey from here. The stone plaza in front of the building itself was hardly lighted except for street lamps half a block away. The water on the leaves caught a glimmer about my feet. The air was chill, windless. I sat down on the edge of the step and ran my feet forward through leaves over stone.

I leaned forward for a moment, and then sat up again. Someone was coming past. A brown coat, hat, the rolling *thunk* of shoes on concrete over the brush and little crunch of wet leaves. I watched him come, and he had passed and was going now, and going, and then brightened beneath a street lamp, and faded out.

I opened the notebook now, and wrote on the top of the page,

"Dear Dad,"

and then I closed the book again. I put my head forward now, resting forehead on crossed arms, looking at the stone beneath my feet. Thought came indistinct and meaningless as the yellow nimbus of the street lamps, words I couldn't understand formed in the river's mouth. There was a dryness in my face, there was no grief, nor was there peace; the air wept for me, and inside the shell of me there was the torrential worrying of waves on black sand. The wet leaves were still and heavy on the pavement. I slept late, the next day. Then, Judith was standing at the door of my room while I turned on my waking arm and shoulder. "Jimmy, you've got to get dressed right away. They want you at the hospital."

"Mother. . . ?" I started.

"You and Margaret have to get ready now. Your mother has already gone."

"All right," I said. I got up, slipped into the envelopment of clothes, while a fist in my stomach opened, pushing stomach and gut and heart away from the growing hollow in its fingers. My sister and I came into the hall from our rooms at a fraction's discrepancy. Our eyes struck each other with bewilderment. We walked down the hall to the door, and waited. Then I said, "Come on. We have to go, now."

"What about Judith?" Margaret asked.

"I guess she's gone already."

"Oh," said Margaret.

We went outside, got into the maroon stiffness of a taxi; then we were out traversing the band of sidewalk between curb and building and then the flickering of our own steps beat the hall tiles.

Getting out of the elevator on my father's floor, we moved into the waves of relatives. His two spinster sisters swayed like gray trees together by the lounge door. Other aunts, other uncles, shuffled by themselves from position through position; some conversed. Faces turned like black and white vanes on a radiometer, toward us, away. Margaret looked silent above the silk knot loose on her neck. With high heels on she was as tall as I was. Relatives veered, turned hands from back to palm under the fluorescent light, and then turned again.

"Do you want to go in and see him now?" an uncle asked. He had put an arm around Margaret's shoulder. Her head wheeled toward him and for a half second back neck muscles beneath held-up-hair were going to say: "Take your hand off me." But suddenly she leaned over against him and cried. Turning faces halted in revolution. It was a very tight, small crying through eyelids creased up like clenched paper. The uncle patted her shoulder. "You don't have to go in," he said.

After a moment, she stood away from him and opened her eyes again, looking at me now. Carefully she rubbed her eyes with her forefingers. Then we went down the hall and into my father's room.

It was full of breath.

The tent, a collapsed bubble hung from a hook over the bed, shook. It took so many pipes and jars and cylinders to inflate the wrecked lung! Mother turned toward us, her face an open bird. The nurse, the same one, still there, sat beside him, adjusting things here, down here, over here about the bed. Dad roared at us from behind the shook plastic. I glanced at my sister: she was smiling, and she raised her hand and waved. She went around on the side of the bed and put her arm around Mom's shoulder. Then she stopped a little and slipped her hand beneath the tent to take his.

"No," the nurse said, quietly.

Margaret shook a little, as though someone had struck the ground she stood on with a sledgehammer, but the smile hugged the muscles of her face. She stepped backward, and waved at him again. The eyes suddenly flew to me. "Hi," I said. "Can you hear me through that this thing?"

I saw the nod.

"Good," I said.

"Don't talk to him," the nurse said. "You mustn't tire him."

"Oh," I said. I stood at the side of the bed and suddenly where his hand lay out against the tent, skin flattened as seen pressed on glass from the wrong side, I took his hand and pressed it: perfect looseness in a double bag of plastic and flesh.

The nurse nodded us out; struck, we left, my sister a little ahead of me. The aunts and the uncles were waiting for us across the hall. And the large one moved to my sister's side. "How is it?" he asked her.

She leaned against him now. And again her face trapped itself closed with the thin wailing of young furies.

We left the hospital together. "I'm going to take a cab home," Margaret said. "You don't have to."

"You got money?" I asked.

"Um-hm."

The day, washed through last night, was winter blue and cool. She walked off the curb, paused before the slugging halt of yellow metal. Then she waved to me out the window. I had already started walking.

5.

Turning up Broadway, I walked in neutral air. It must be Sunday, I thought. The closed doors of bars held in chittering music, like mouthfuls of dry sand. A radio rested silent in a window.

The trees on the island that divided the way dropped bands of shadow across my side of the street. I could see Julliard, down beyond the gothic crinkle of Union Theological Seminary's gray and white stone walls. On Sunday, the sound from the practice conservatory was not so loud. My fists swung in the bottom of my coat pockets. The sidewalk here was lightly graveled and swished with low stepping.

She was turning from the walk to the gray cube when I saw her. She held her coat open with a hand in each pocket, a gray coat that cleared to a thick black and white weave as I came nearer, recognizing her.

"Hello, Niva."

"Jimmy!" She smiled, came forward, and stopped in front of me. Then she took a step back. "My God. I haven't seen you since *years*! You live just down the block, too. You know, that's obscene."

"You don't live around here," I said.

"No. But I'm at Juilliard now."

"Oh," I said. "Still with the piano?"

"Um-hm," she said. "Do you still see anybody, you know, from school?"

"I just ran into Geo," I said. "In fact I'll probably be seeing him at the end of this week."

"Geo Keller?" she asked, with a strange tilting of voice and face.

"He's married now, you know? You remember him."

"I remember him," she said. "Yes, I know. I was always very fond of him. I hope his wife is too. He can be intolerable at times. I've never met her. They had a party right after they were married, and I got an invitation through Jake Lewin, but I couldn't make it. As a matter of fact, Jake gave the party for them. I wanted to come down later, and Jake and I were going to get together, but I had to leave for school and the whole thing got balled up; so I never saw them."

"Who's Jake?" I asked.

"You know him," said Niva with gentle incredulity. "Or maybe you don't. He was a year before you, perhaps. No, two years ahead of me. I guess that's why you never knew him." Then she stopped. "What have you been doing?"

"You're away at school?" I asked.

"Um-hm," she said. "This is only a summer course at Julliard. It's just about over now. Come on, where are you coming from?"

"The hospital," I said.

"You're not sick, are you?"

"My father is," I said.

"Is it serious?" she asked.

I reached up and rubbed at my ear. "He's going to die," I said.

The muscles of her face opened, cheek, forehead, jaw. "Oh, Jimmy . . ." she said with a slowing of breath. She had taken her hands out of her pockets.

"Everyone is sitting around waiting," I said. "They shouldn't let people die like this. They shouldn't let people have time to do what they're doing. People shouldn't have time to mourn."

She nodded, slightly. "What's happening at your house?"

"Everyone's getting ready for mourning. They're going around like he was dead already. People shouldn't be given time to do that."

"I don't know what I'm supposed to say," she said. "How long?"

"Days, I guess," I said. "Who the hell knows. They thought it was weeks before. But it's gotten worse."

"Has he been ill long?"

"Months," I said. "Lung cancer. It's eating up his breathing in little left bent circles. Do you remember what the cells look like under a microscope?"

"Don't talk about things like that, now," she said. "You're very upset."

"Am I?" I asked.

"Yes."

"I'm angry," I said. "I'm angry that it should happen to people. Mourning before breakfast. You shouldn't do it on an empty stomach."

"Why be like that," she said. "Come on and walk with me."

We started in sudden silence.

"You weren't going in this direction before," I said.

"I thought we could go back to the Julliard cafeteria and have some coffee."

"Oh."

We turned into the walk, approached the gray wall and the open, single, black-framed door, and sank into the building with the mounting of a double step like bright silver balls dropped in gray cement.

The halls were dark and the stone steps worn heavily in the middle. "Like in Geo's halls," I said.

"Oh?" asked Niva with a smile. "The building isn't that old, this one anyway."

"Maybe stone goes through quickly," I said.

The cafeteria was closed.

"Oh, I forgot," said Niva. "It's Sunday. Maybe you'd better go on home. I just thought it would be nice to sit down together for a little while, though."

"Are any of the practice rooms open?" I asked.

"Probably," she said.

"Will you play something?"

"O.K." We started up the hall. "I remember once sitting under a piano when a friend of mine was playing Rachmaninoff. In fact there were three of us under the piano. This was a guy who could whip off ten or twenty concerti from one end to the other without a slip. Rachmaninoff is very hard to take from under the piano. You can't really hear any of the mistakes in it, in the music or the playing. But you come out feeling purged."

People had stuck little slips of paper in the doors of the practice rooms to signify occupancy. We opened one door, and a young man jumped on the piano stool inside, and said, "Oh, I'm sorry. Did my slip fall out?"

"That's all right," said Niva. And closed the door. "It isn't usually crowded on Sunday. I guess we'll go somewhere else."

Then she looked at me, worried almost. "Do you really want to stay?"

"Yes," I said.

"All right," and she smiled.

The room we did find was large, blue, and filled with two grand pianos.

"*Ohhhhh*," said Niva. "You know, I forgot this place existed. I haven't been here in years. Have I ever been up here?" she suddenly asked. "Maybe it was another room. You don't play?" she asked.

"No."

"That's a shame. We'd do a duet."

She touched a few notes on one. "It's in tune. My God!" She slipped onto the bench, stood up again, raised the slab of shiny wood, laying back its brass and silver gut to frosted light from the opaque windows, sat down once more and bent over three chorded swells of sound. I sat down on the floor and slid underneath the high body and closed my eyes. She played one note, and it struck my head full like a glass sphere filled with water. She played another one, too verberately close to the first to distinguish the interval; another, another, and the number lost itself in the heaviness of felted sound, and chain of notes, links thick with distance, soft by extended overtone. My head shook and my eyelids filled up with beads of music. Then she stopped.

Someone was saying, "Excuse me. I think I have the room during this hour."

"Oh," said Niva. "I'm sorry."

I stood up from under the piano. A young man in a blue serge suit and dark tie looked at me with surprise from where his too-small, too-round face balanced on his Windsor knot.

Niva and I left the room. “Well,” she said.

As we were leaving the building, I asked her, “Have you ever heard the carillons over at Riverside Church?”

“Sometimes I hear them when I’m around here.”

“I mean from up close, inside the church, right under them.”

“No,” she said. “I haven’t.”

“Oh,” I said.

6.

Unoccupied rooms are filled with dark disuse, beds made in acquiescence to ritual, that no matter what the emergency, order will be maintained, pajamas hung up, dresser tops kept neat; my sister kept to her room, I to mine.

When the doorbell rang, both my sister and I came to answer it. I opened the door. Sound burst through like a black bubble of tattered wailing, cloth and raised hands. They supported my crying mother and wailing aunts. “It’s all over. It’s all over,” someone unrecognizable turned face to me and said — Judith — ”He didn’t feel any pain at all. It’s all over now.”

My mother, through their hands, crying, tried to go toward the living room. An uncle grabbed my arm and put it around someone’s shoulder, a black clad elder aunt. And someone shoved Margaret toward my mother so that she nearly fell against her. Somehow the welling group veered between my sister and I, and across their turning, lowering heads that gathered like black moths about my mother on the couch, we looked at each other, with reverberating puzzlement. All the women, my mother, and even my sister, were wearing black, whether by custom or morbid precognition, I suddenly did not care to guess. The loose, silken knot at Margaret's throat was green, from the shadows half a room away, emeralds, parrot's wing, or apple leaves.

Later that evening, I flipped through the old brown leather telephone book beneath the lamp. Niva's number was there, and I called her.

"Hello?" she said.

"This is Jimmy," I said. "He died. This afternoon."

She waited a long time. Then she said, "Oh. I can't think of anything to say, except maybe it's good it's over, for you."

"Maybe," I said. "Yes. I guess I shouldn't have called you. But I just felt like it."

"Then you should have," she said. "It's all right."

"I just wanted to tell you." Silence. "Goodbye. Can I see you sometime soon, maybe."

"I go back to school in two days," she said. "And I've only got tomorrow really free."

"I don't think I can get out tomorrow," I said. "Well, I just wanted to say something."

"I know," said Niva. "You can say good-bye now, and it'll be all right."

"Thank you," I said. "Good-bye."

"Good-bye."

III. The City

> "... Your eyes are an inscription in my hand
> that reads my face and tells me what I am ...
> A move complements a move. As games are
> played, if I betray, you are the one betrayed."[164]
>
> — Marilyn Hacker

1.

Fire wound slow changing rivers on the late sky as we rounded the corner. "What is that?" Margaret asked.

---

[164] Excerpted from "The Terrible Children," by Marilyn Hacker, written c. 1958.

"I remember when they were tearing down buildings in this neighborhood," I said, "when I came to see him last time. I think this was one of the blocks they demolished."

"Then they're burning it off now," Margaret said.

Two flattened blocks flickered before us, infernal breath against heavy blue. I glanced at Margaret's face, and saw shadow roll over it, light, and shadow. "With this neighborhood, they could really burn the whole thing down and not miss any of it. Geo lives in a rat trap."

She turned to me. "Has he changed much?"

"I don't think so," I said.

"I wonder what his wife is like?"

"So do I."

We walked across the street from the fire. Behind it, the taller buildings at Fourteenth Street burned in their own yellow and mute orange: pale windows, illuminated clock faces, searchlights, a gothic indentured faded stone above and behind the flames which cut sharply into indigo.

"Mom is going to be angry," I said.

Margaret said quietly, "Why?"

"Because it's so soon after. She doesn't think we should go out."

"She doesn't think we should go out for a year and a day," Margaret said. "The first time we went, no matter when it was, she'd get mad. It might as well be now."

"It was last night," I said. "The funeral."

"It seems a lot longer," she said.

"I'm tired."

"So am I."

Then we went around the corner and the turning wall wiped out the flame, and at the same time slipped back revealing the broken wall of the slum street that sank before us, littered and crowded, down the evening.

From street to hall was from twilight into night: "The place smells," I said.

"Not that much," Margaret said. "What floor?"

"The third one. I think I remember this is it."

I knocked. Then I twisted the paint-thick wing key at breast level, and a bell screamed in the dark. Light cut up and down the edge of the door jamb and a head moved through the yellow line. Then the door sailed completely opened, and Geo said, "Well, come in. You're the first to get here."

"We got your wife's invitation," Margaret said, stepping in ahead of me. I followed.

"You even beat her here." He stepped back for us. "How's your father getting along?"

"He died," I said.

In the following silence, I got a chance to see the blotches of plaster on the kitchen walls. Plaster, when it gets wet, festers into a feathery brown fungoid excrescence the texture of dried, blistered shaving foam. Wood from which the linoleum has been ripped shows blotched glue stains and grain marked with encrusted filth.

When it was getting uncomfortably silent," I said, "Let's go inside. When do we eat?" There were pots on the stove.

"Things are cooking," Geo said, pointing to them. "I guess when Laile gets here."

"Anyone else coming besides us?" I asked.

"My wife, I hope," said Geo. "And Paul. Daniele, who you don't know, is also coming. And afterwards I think we're going to be descended upon by some friends of mine who have been instructed to descend about nine o'clock."

We followed Margaret into the living room. She stood in the center now, tall, wrapped in the black dustiness of her dress, looking around the room.

"Well," Geo said, when she finally faced us again. "How do you like it?"

There was an indifference like marble over her face.

"It's still got to be painted. And it could be cleaner. Though not much; I Cloroxed the floors today. That's why it smells a little strange, maybe."

Finally I said, "It looks O.K."

Margaret sat down in a chair.

"Admitted," Geo continued to her, "it's not much. I guess you're not too impressed, huh?"

I thought of ice turning into a glass of water, and then marble broke with small fissures of her laughter. "Are you very concerned with what I think of it?" she asked.

Geo put his hands in his back pockets, dropped his head, and then looked up with pursed lips. "No," he said.

"Good," Margaret said, leaning back.

Geo laughed.

Halfway through the sound, Margaret's face caught at his, and it stopped.

"You have books," she said. "You always had books. Where are they?"

"You want to read now?" Geo asked. "What have you been doing? How are things? Where are you in school? What do you want to be when you grow up?" Hands still in back pockets, he ended the question in a sort of amused whimsy.

"I've been doing nothing. I'm in my junior year of high school, and I don't like it; and more than likely I shall not grow up. Where are your books?"

Geo shrugged. "In there." He shouldered toward a door, at the room's side.

Margaret got up quickly from the chair, started away, but turned back. Then she grinned: "Thank you?" and tilted her head. After that she left the room.

I followed Geo into the kitchen, and ended up leaning against the side of the door, too distracted by his culinary puttering as he seasoned and tasted and boiled and poured, to talk. I was just about to give up and sit down in the living room again when the bell sheered through my head.

"Get that for me?" Geo said, steam from a lifted pot lid suddenly around his ears.

I stood up from my lounging, and opened the door. She was a hefty girl in blue jeans and a red zipper jacket. No, not so much hefty as without contour of either waist or breast. Her hair was cut very short, a color between honey and sand. She smiled, said, "Hello. Am I in the right place?" and then looked around me into the kitchen. "Oh," she added. "Hi, Geo," and waved. "Where's Laile?"

"Oh, Daniele, Jimmy; Jimmy, Daniele."

"She's not here yet," Geo said as the girl came in.

We shook hands, and as hands dropped, another figure moved outside the door, stepped inside. A nodded head, "Daniele."

"Hi, Paul."

"Geo, Jimmy." Then the tall boy, fading to familiarity, edged past and went into the living room. He called back, "Paul, do you have a copy of *The Notebooks of Malte Laurids Brigge*?"

"Second shelf from the top near the left," said Geo. Then he said, "God damn lending library. Close the door, Jimmy, before they find what they want and run off with it. We can't eat all this food ourselves!"

"I'm hungry," said Daniele. "Can I have a glass of milk?"

"Icebox."

"Where's Laile?" Daniele asked again, disappearing behind the icebox door.

"I don't know," Geo said, putting a lid down on a pot. "I don't know." His shirt cuffs were rolled above his elbows, and sometimes as he jammed his hands into his pockets so that the rusted patch of skin there, in bending, would expand to a regular color. "When I went out this morning, she was here. I came back, she wasn't."

Suddenly he whirled around and presented me with an onion and a small knife. "Dice."

"I'll cry," I said.

"Then cry," and he made room for me by him at the sink.

"Is there anything I can do?" asked Daniele.

"You want to dice an onion?" I asked.

"Sure," she said, moving in to take my place.

"You," said Geo, not looking at me, "are the laziest son of a bitch I know. All you ever do is stand around and let things happen to you. You know that? Don't you ever do anything?"

"What's your problem?" Daniele asked Geo. "So he doesn't want to cry." She sniffed. "Can you blame him?" Then she sniffed twice. "Are you worried about Laile?" she asked.

Geo shrugged and looked into another kettle. "I'm ready for the onion," he said.

"Just a minute," Daniele said. "Here we go." She handed him the saucer of wet white chips which he emptied into the steamy pot.

I turned back to the living room.

Margaret and Paul had just come from the book room. The three of us entered together, and for a moment stopped and watched each other. Paul was wearing black pants and a white shirt with his cuffs turned up once. He was holding a book in one hand.

"Hi, Paul," I said. "I haven't seen you in years."

"Margaret, do you know Paul?"

"Yeah," she said. She reached up and unknotted the green scarf from her neck, a noose of beryl fire in the inadequate light. Then she left Paul's side and took a seat.

Paul looked down at the book, and began to turn pages. Then he said, "This is the passage," and held it out to her. She extended her arm, but they were on opposite sides of the room. Neither one moved for the attenuation of seconds, and then, synchronously, Paul stepped forward, and Margaret rose from her chair, the green scarf sliding over her black skirt and onto the floor. She took the book, sat down again and bent over it. Paul went to the couch, stretched out on his stomach and folded his hands under his cheek, face to the wall.

From the kitchen I heard Geo say: "Where the hell is my silly wife?"

I turned from the living room's silence back into the kitchen.

"She'll get here," Daniele was saying. "You don't have to worry about her."

"I'm not worried," said Geo. He glanced over his shoulder as I came. "What's going on in there?" he asked.

"Nothing. Margaret's reading. Paul's gone to sleep."

"That's a great way to greet an old friend," Geo said.

Daniele said: "How long are you going to wait. I'm starved."

Geo turned toward me. "Will you look at the alarm clock on the table in the living room?"

I ducked back in. Margaret's scarf was now in a crumple of green on Paul's shoulder where he lay unmoved. It was eight o'clock.

"Well, that's an hour after she invited you for," Geo said. "Lobster tails under the broiler, then. And that's it."

"Lobster tails?" I asked. "What are we having?"

Ka-klank of icebox door; *schrundle-trundle* of opening stove broiler, and Daniele ferried a tray, foiled in bright aluminum, with naked tails of lobster, past me, onto the broiling pan, and then *schrundle-trundle* again.

"Daniele, you know where silver and stuff is. Do you want to set things out."

"Sure," Daniele answered, and was by me out into the living room. I wandered out, side-stepped Daniele who came at me, oblivious with handfuls of cutlery, and at last went into the dark room in which my sister and Paul had been. Box-like shelves, with two compartments were piled up one wall to the ceiling. There was a filing cabinet by one wall, and piles of books by another. On one of the shelves there was a heap of notebooks, their cardboard covers smudged both by hands and the room's shadow. I picked up the top one and ruffled pages which turned over into poems, prose, lists of figures; and once I stopped where across two pages were scribbled obliquely, a shopping list. Moving to a window, I opened the first page again. It said,

GEO KELLER
Notes & Journals

followed by a late summer date, and a year that suddenly added an age to both me and the book. Geo had been eighteen when he started this.

A few pages into it ". . . . at the Banquet that evening, Mr. Sloan sat very straight down the long table. I watched most of the evening at the side. There was Frost, sitting near the center dais; He looked like a thing made of gouged lard stuck on the collar and in the sleeves of a big baggy suit. There was candle light wrapping itself around the columns of the room. There was a warmth of fine wood; and later, Mr. Ciardi made a speech that rang through with the sounds of affection as well as the drunken disdain I had found in him as far back as the evening when at the party he had come in slightly high with Gloria into Herbert's and my room where we were singing. Completely oblivious to what we sang, he rocked into some deep song he had once listened to all night long, years ago. Somebody once said that Ciardi looked more like a truck driver than a poet.

"Later, representing the scholars, Gloria, a brown moth with antenna dipped in vitriol, stood up and made a somewhat strange speech concerning freedom and racial equality. Ciardi, I remember, had introduced her as one of the most meteoric poets of today. Mr. Frost finally took his bow, to an ovation that rose like waves, a suddenly standing hoard, all through the room, until the elderly, deafening man could not be seen at all. Julia Sloan, a monument to the practicality of a certain Western Strain, regardless of the tradition of greatness into which I sometimes felt some of these dog-toothed were attempting to thrust Frost, took the old man by the arm (She towers over him by a foot), helped him from his chair, and turned him around to see the standing people. I thought of the Contralto soloist turning the deaf Beethoven to see the applause of the audience at the premiere of the 9th symphony.

"Another memory of Judith Sloan, standing on the lawn like trees, like waves; and the trees blowing in a sudden gust. And Dave whispering to me, later that night down at the beer party in the winter ski-cabin, 'Mrs. Sloan is a poem.'

"It was after the Banquet that Julia Sloan surged over to me, a sort of mirthful Venus from behind the waves of club women who seemed a sea in themselves. She grabbed my shoulder and cried, "Come. Come, here. I want you to meet Mr. Frost." And I was towed across the room like a skier by a motor-boat through rough water. I had somehow forgotten what she had said before about giving a sheaf of poetry to him. It seemed that the farce — and though I was the only one who thought of it as such, still it seemed a farce — of the reaction to the reading from my work the previous week was turning like broken mirrors.

"We moored into the immediate crowd which was standing around Frost. Julia supported him again, having wrapped that protective sunbeam about her face which she used to deploy crowds in a manner well suited for Helen of Troy. The dark hulk of Mr. Ciardi shadowed behind them. Julia reached toward me and suddenly I was pulled in front of him.

"'Mr. Frost[165], this is the young man whose poetry you read.'

"He was shorter than I. Julia was smiling. The string of his hearing aid was pink down into his pocket. Mr. Ciardi had moved up and was smiling too. 'I'm very glad to meet you,' I said, roaring through the thousand vices around us and the impressions flooding me, like the feel of his limp fleshed hand.

"Silence; he smiled. 'I'm glad to meet you,' he said. 'You have strength. You have a lot to learn, but do it your way. Don't let them tell you how to do it.'

"Then Ciardi was saying something to Julia about Mr. Frost being tired, and the club women were being shooed off, and then they drew him back and away, and Julia Sloan turned once around and was beside her husband, tall, and perhaps a little disapproving of her extravagance in showing my poems to Mr. Frost. And if he didn't think it an extravagance, at any rate, I certainly did.

"Later, that evening, through the whirl of parties that grew, blistered, and metastasized across the hill, Nancy and Dave and

---

[165] The incident above is based on something that happened at the Bread Loaf Writers' Conference in Middlebury, VT, where the poet Robert Frost and the poet John Ciardi were in July 1960 and Samuel Delany had a work-scholarship as a waiter. Julia was Julia Sloan, wife of the publisher William Sloan.

Herb all gathered around me and asked what had happened. As the youngsters of the entire affair, we would cluster, break, and cluster again through those nights. I told them, and Nancy had the most pragmatic and at once romantic comment to make: 'I think that's very good for you,' she said. . . ."

From the living room Paul's voice called, "Jimmy, come on out and eat."

As I emerged, Geo was saying, "My house is not a library, damn it. Paul, get up off the couch and be civil. Margaret, put that book down." He placed on the table a huge broiling tray heaped with yellow rice, a gumbo thick with shrimp, black olives, beans, chick peas, chicken, and edged by a pile of crisped lobster tails, just the rims of their red shells blackened, their white, pink-veined bellies shining with butter.

"All that for five people?"

"There were supposed to be six."

"Don't worry about Laile," Daniele said.

"I'm not worried," Geo said. "I'm not even annoyed. I just wish, God damn it, she was here."

We say down (the dinner was buffet since there was no table big enough to hold us all in the house) and received plates of steaming gumbo of saffron rice and two broiled lobster tails. Daniele, playing hostess, poured us paper cups of sauterne, and a sluggish conversation bloomed quietly over warm food and wine.

When we were finished, Margaret and I volunteered to wash dishes. I turned around from the sink once to put a stack of dishes on the ice box top, and saw Paul quietly leaning against the door-way where I had been before; Margaret's green scarf was balled up in his fist.

Inside, Geo was talking to Daniele: "Well, shall we wait for her?"

"She'd just think you were doing it to make her feel bad," Daniele said. "Which, if you did, it would be."

"That's not true," Geo said.

"Yes it is," Daniele said. "I know you."

"She didn't seem in the sort of 'I'm not coming back mood' she gets into sometimes."

"Did you have an argument?"

"No," Geo said. "No; we didn't."

"You know she's not particularly fond of Loupo and the rest of them."

"I'm not particularly fond of them," Geo said. "But I think they're funny. I don't think she'd cut out just to avoid them. Besides, she could stay home. We weren't going to stay around here."

"You'd be crazy if you did," Daniele said. "I wouldn't let them in my house for five minutes. I'd turn around and find they'd taken everything that wasn't nailed down."

"I know," Geo said. "I hope something hasn't happened to her."

"I don't think so," Daniele said. "I really don't."

The dish towel had gotten soggy by the last pot-top. Closing kitchen cabinet doors flung across the light. Geo seemed nervous at his absent wife; I was curious, and yet the extent of his nervousness, from his tones to Daniele as they talked in the other room, did not peak me further than to acknowledge that my curiosity was there and somewhat unsatisfied. My stomach, more than full, was far easier to concentrate on than on vanished Laile. When we finished sweeping, moving chairs, clearing the ice-box top and so forth, Paul handed Margaret back the scarf, silently, with only the white extension of his arm.

She took his whole hand, and for an instant, the green silk ball was the nadir of an ivory/onyx catenary: Margaret's black dress had long sleeves buttoning at her wrist.

"Come on," Geo said. "Let's go out for a walk."

I was going to say something about his friends' coming, but I guessed he wanted to avoid them. A look from Daniele silenced the comment I might have made; and in a swish and rustle of coats and jackets, we were out of the apartment into the filthy hall. My sister and Paul led down the steps, followed by Daniele's stocky jouncings. Geo walked with me.

The hall light was out, and so we passed into darkness on the steps. "Hey," I said to Geo, as we came out into the twilit lower hallway; "When did you meet Robert Frost?"

"Huh?" asked Geo. "A couple years ago, I think. Why?"

"I was browsing in one of your old journals."

"Oh," said Geo. "Find anything juicy?"

"No," I said. "Should I have looked further?"

"You know that's not very polite."

"I'm sorry."

"Oh, that's O.K.," Geo said. "I'd mind with anyone else but you, and my wife, and maybe one or two other people."

"For a moment I felt unique," I said.

We came out on the street, night-toned now, steel grays and deep graphites, blues hushed to the color of old tires, worn tarpaper, and slashes of velvet.

"I'm sorry about your father's death," Geo said. "Which doesn't mean anything. But I am."

"Why?"

"Because of you. Because of what it's probably put you through already and what it will put you through in the future."

"What's that mean?"

"Not too much, I suppose. My father isn't dead yet, so I really don't know."

"Are you angry about the journal?"

"No writer, no person, probably, ever puts on paper what he sincerely doesn't want read — a few years after his death at any rate."

"Well, you're not dead yet."

"Give me time," said Geo. "Just give me time."

"You're really depressed."

"You're observant," Geo said. "Did you know that you were depressed too?"

"I didn't."

"That's bad," Geo said. "Because you are."

"I guess this is sort of a depressant evening," I mused. "Paul hasn't said anything all evening and Margaret's been reading."

"I don't think it's depression with them," Geo said. "I don't think they ever really get depressed."

"What do they do?"

"That's a good question," Geo said.

We turned the corner and expanding before us now was the glowing stretch of incended wrecks. We all drew up, halted before it. "That's impressive," said Daniele.

In some places fire lashed twenty feet into the night, at others, black hanks of cinders looped the earth. Once a breeze came as one of these and black snakes blew away revealing glowing coals. There were hillocks and dells of broken brick and rubbish. There was no edge to it, either. The cracked sidewalk dropped directly, perhaps a foot, onto the arena.

It was Margaret who first started out into the rubble of the field. We watched without comment. When she had gone about twenty feet, she stopped beside a bush of fire, and stood in silhouette before a greater flame, a golden geyser fifty feet ahead. Paul stepped out next, walking through a series of bright highlights that slashed at him again and again. He stopped behind Margaret, a little below her and to the side. Daniele, Geo and I stood at the edge and only watched. Then we heard the wailing, suddenly. A high, hysterical scream; then someone laughed, very far away; and I was for the first time aware of the tremendous sound the flames were making, a steady roar like the seas, without pulse or swell, though.

Miniature black figures, far off were running. They came, darting around fire, leaping over coal beds, stopping, changing direction. Four, no five. They spread, and then converged, still without faces or definite sex, about Paul and Margaret. It was at this point that I ran about ten steps into the field. Then something happened: a little one, maybe the leader, brushed past Margaret, who stepped back. Instantly, Paul sprang forward and grabbed him; the two whirled in outline, and the little one screeched. Then Paul was marching him toward us, one arm jammed up behind his back. Margaret followed him.

When they reached us, Paul shoved his charge toward Geo. "Here's your friend," he said.

The figure lost its balance, and then snapped back into it like a quivering rubber man. He whirled a brilliant head around toward Paul: "Cut that shit out," he snapped.

"What were you supposed to be doing? Geo asked.

"Running," the figure said, whirling its head back toward Paul (something gold flashed at the ear). "Cut that out, you hear me?"

He — and the sex defined itself only after seconds — was thin, taut bodied, and tight waisted, in a pair of black Levis that could have been painted on. He wore filthy tennis sneakers and stood with his feet wide apart. His hair was redder than the fire, long, combed once meticulously, but shaking loose. His shirt, electric blue, was opened halfway down a pallid cage of bone. The gold at the side of his head was a circular earring.

"Loupo; Jimmy, Margaret," Geo said.

He looked at me, and grinned. "Hello, baby," he said, and grinned. He jerked around toward Margaret, and whistled. "Hello!"

Margaret laughed. When he turned back, I saw he was still smiling.

Out of the silhouette another boy came, taller, also wispier. He had a mop of blond silk which he would suddenly stop and fling back from his face. "Billy," Geo said. "And you, little one," he nodded toward Daniele. "Oh, hello," he said, looking from myself to Margaret. He carried his wrists as if they were tied by not-quite-long-enough strings around his neck. There was nothing indefinite about his sex; he was exactly mid-way.

I glanced at the other three, expecting to see something more or less of the same genre. The next boy who came loping up seemed out of place. He was six feet plus a handful of inches, dark, and barrel boned. He had black leather boots on, that came above mid-shin where faded blue jeans disappeared behind metal buckles. His hair was black, thick, and shiny; his face, burnished mahogany, his hands were long, roped with veins, and the nails clean and curved. Flame caught them, and for an instant I thought of *David's* hand on the Michelangelo statue, recarved in terra cotta.

"Oona," Geo said, continuing introductions, "Helen," and I realized one of them was a girl, "and Joe."

"What are you doing out here?" Oona, the giant, asked Paul. "I thought we were supposed to come over to Geo's house."

"We came to intercept you," Paul said.

"They were cutting out on us, beautiful," Loupo told Oona. "Cut them." He rubbed his arm where Paul had twisted it.

"Hi, Daniele," the girl, Helen, said. "Where's Laile?"

"Not here," answered Daniele.

Helen rubbed at her nose with her fist. She was wearing suede pants and jacket. The light, through her disarranged and electric hair, tinged auburn what was probably a coffee and cream brown. "Oh," said Helen. Now she rubbed her eyes. "Soot," she said. "Loupo, you're crazy."

"It's part of my charm, baby face," retorted Loupo. The remaining boy, ambling, yet with ursine grace, even darker than Oona, came over to me, unzipped his motorcycle jacket in a jingling of loose buckles, grinned, and said, "What's your name again?"

"Jimmy," I said.

"Hey there," he said, giving me a heavy-handed but playful whack on the shoulder. "I'm Joe."

"Hello," I said. "Come on, let's get out of here," said Loupo.

Margaret had already started off through the field again slender and black against the white-orange. Suddenly Billy, in a flurry of his own ash-blond hair scampered after her. Reaching her, he pranced along beside until she looked at him and laughed. Billy looked over his shoulder at the rest of us and giggled. Margaret took his hand, and at first you could see him jump, but then they went on, quietly, far enough away now so that their swaying forms shivered with intervening heat.

"Come on, Oona," Paul said. He started off first. And the tall boy came, waves of light rolling back over the crown of his hair and the planes of his face.

Once Paul stooped, caught up a burning stick, and whirled around in front of the following giant. He swatted the stick on the ground and then hurled it into the air; involuntarily, Oona leaped back from the ascendant tower of sparks flung up between them, crouched, and covered his eyes. "Come on, you big bastard," Paul yelled, laughing. "Come on."

The stick came down in sparks beside Oona, who took a plunging step onward. "Hey . . ." he bellowed.

"Come on," laughed Paul.

Behind me, I heard Loupo's slow, high chuckling.

"Is he an Indian?" I asked Joe, who was still beside me. I meant Oona.

Joe shrugged and zippers jingled. "I don't know." He gave me another whack on the shoulder. "Come on." And we started off behind them.

Helen and Daniele walked to our side, and then got ahead of us. In step, loping, their walks sped each other and yet were different. Helen, the soft brown of her clothes and hair, the sway of her body, animal beside Daniele's short haired waistless figure. Daniele reached out and put her arm around Helen's shoulder, who moved closer, and then dug her little finger vigorously in her ear. "This damn soot," she said.

"Close up the God damn ranks," Loupo cried. "Come on, speed up," he added, shoving me and Joe.

Flame wound around us. Soot blew at us once, and heat struck the sides of our faces, and then cold. Stretched out at the start, now we clotted in the fire. The city burned away behind the flames, and sky, once I looked up, was very close and black.

Billy, in a high breathless, ash-blond voice, was in the midst of telling my sister some immensely complicated story which she seemed to be paying fairly close attention to ". . . and then she said to me, but of course I didn't let her go any further than the first couple of words, the *first* couple of words, I tell you . . ." when Loupo called;

"Shut up you God damn pansy."

Beside me, Joe giggled. "Where are we going?" I asked Joe, to make talk, since he seemed friendly.

He shrugged. "I dunno."

"But we'll have one hell of a time getting there, hey?" Loupo bawled.

"Yeah," said Geo, dryly.

Paul, near the front of the group, yelled back at us, "Hey, I bet nobody can jump over that."

"Jump over what?" Geo asked.

A snake of fire hedged flickering orange three feet high.

"I can jump that," Daniele said. "I bet."

"Come on," Geo said. "It's dangerous enough in here without anybody doing something foolish."

"That's not high."

"I bet it'll be hot going over, though."

"Forget it," Geo said. "Let's get out of here. Where we going, huh?"

"How about cutting over to the village?" Daniele said. "After I jump over this, huh?" She started walking backward.

"Come on," Helen said. "You'll burn yourself." Daniele pushed her back with one hand and elbowed Billy aside with the other. Suddenly she ran forward (away from us, toward the flame), sprang, and hovered instantly on the black, limbs crouched, whipped with light. Then her legs shot down, and I thought she would land in the fire. But she cleared, and went running forward, and the night clapped to behind her like a door.

"That wasn't hard," we heard her call back to us.

"I can get over," said Paul. "Hey, Oona, you go first."

"Huh?" laughed the big framed boy. "Uh-uhh, not me."

"Come on," said Paul. "It isn't high."

"I got other things to do than burn my ass," Oona said.

Daniele approached from the other side of the fire. The light bright under her chin, below her ears, her nose, and her eyes caves of shadow. "It's not hard," she said. "And you don't feel it going over. And it isn't even warm."

"God damn," said Oona. "Leave me alone."

"I bet you could even do it," Paul turned to my sister.

"In this dress?" said Margaret.

"You look like you could be a good jumper," Daniele said to Oona from across the wall of flame. "Those long legs you got."

"Watch out," said Oona.

"Hey look," said Geo. "Don't let him make you do something. . ."

"Nobody's making me do nothing," Oona said. He lunged back, flung forward, and legs and arms hurtled into a knot above the fire.

Paul threw his head back, suddenly, and laughed, a loud, shocking laugh, on a strange pitch that made me start to look at him. Only I didn't, because at the sound, Oona's legs snapped down onto the earth like jack hammers. Only he was going too fast to stop and lunged forward through the fire.

"Hey," said Loupo, after a second.

Then Daniele's voice from the other side of the light said, "What the hell is the matter with you?" And then, "Are you O.K.?"

We sprinted around the hedge of flame. On the other side, Oona and Daniele were standing. Oona was very stiff, hands in fists. "You all right, beautiful?" Loupo asked. "You're too pretty to get burned."

"God damn," Oona finally said. "What the hell you wanna do that for?" and he turned to Paul.

"Do what?" asked Paul.

I saw Geo turn and give Paul a disgusted look.

"Hey, I'm sorry," said Paul. "I didn't do anything on purpose. How'd you think it exploded?"

"I dunno," Oona said. "I closed my eyes. I couldn't see."

"How was I to know you were gonna close your eyes?" said Paul.

"I'm supposed to keep 'em open when I jump over that?" He thumbed back to the fire.

"I just wanted to see what . . ."

"Let's get out of here, huh?" Geo interrupted, "before we all fry."

Loupo walked by and took Oona's arm. "Did anyone ever tell you you were pretty, Alcibiades?" he said.

"Huh?" said Oona. "Hey, cut that shit out," and he shook Loupo away from him. But we had started moving again. As we neared the edge, suddenly Joe reached down and swiped something up from the ground.

"What's that?" I asked him.

He turned it over in the lessening light. "I donno," he said. It's a scarf. Hey isn't it that girl's?" He pointed ahead to my sister.

The bright crumpled green creased between the fingers of his dark hand.

"Oh," I said. "Yeah. She must have dropped it."

We crossed over onto the far sidewalk now, grayed as if it had all been blown with charcoal dust, in our flame diminished eyes; the buildings, the broken stoops, the shafted fixtures of the dull lamps. Behind me, Loupo and Geo had gotten into a conversation about somebody who wasn't there, while Oona had started again with Paul; it began seriously, but then he reached down and pushed Paul's head, and then they were both laughing and talking about something else.

"Hey Joe," I said. "What are all these people doing here anyway?"

His long face swiveled toward me in the dusted dark. "I donno," he said. "What do you mean?" He flung one hand up into his mass of black hair and combed it twice with his fingers. Then he reached down and scratched his stomach.

"I mean it's sort of a funny group," I said.

Joe looked around. "Yeah," he said. "It is." Then he shrugged once more in the metallic clink of buckles and zipper tabs, and dropped his hands into the bags of his pockets. "What are you doing here?"

"Huh?"

"You tell me what you're here for."

"I don't know," I said. "My father died day before yesterday. And I just wanted to get out for a while."

"Your father died?"

"Um-huh," I said.

"Oh," said Joe. "I never had a father. Least I don't think so."

"You mean he died before you were young?"

"Maybe," Joe said. "Maybe before I was born." Then he laughed. "No, you see, it's like this. I don't got no real parents any more. This woman see, adopted me. I lived with her and her husband up till a year ago; then I went out on my own. Only I got adopted all over again."

"How?" I asked.

"Well, it wasn't really adopted. I was eighteen then, so I was too old. I got in a fight, once, when I wasn't living with anybody or any place. A guy, real old guy too, got cut up bad, and I think maybe died. I think maybe I killed him, too. But there was a lot of other people in the fight. And some of them got hurt pretty bad also; and everybody who was left got sent to court."

"What was the fight about?"

"Hell, I don't know," Joe said. "I just wanted to fight. And it wasn't really bad, cause I think they were real crooks. Anyway, this judge, she was a woman judge, too; she got us up and asked all sorts of questions. She gave a big speech, and then asked me all sorts of things, like, Didn't I realize I wasn't a little boy, and didn't I realize I was a young man now, and didn't I realize I would soon be an old man, and all about society. Women are like that, I guess; because I think a judge ought to say go to hell, and put you in jail, or say go home, and let that be it, instead of asking all those questions. Anyway, I said I realized I was me, Joe; only that didn't shut her up, and I guess she thought I was maybe being smart alecky. But I got off, and all of a sudden this bitch up and wants to adopt me."

"The judge?" I asked.

"No, another one. She wants to take charge of me, she says. So I was entrusted. She lives in a real swell house, and it's all white and pink and it's got real silver spoons and forks. You ever seen real silver?"

I nodded.

"Then you know what I mean," Joe said. And whistled. "Any way, she gives me this long story about how she lost a little boy, years ago, when she was just a kid, a baby. And then her husband died; that was just recently. And it was real sad, and I fell for it. She wasn't bad looking either. Maybe forty-five. She said how she wanted a son and all." Suddenly he put his hand on my shoulder and leaned over and giggled. "You know what she really wanted, though, huh?"

"What?" I asked.

Joe laughed. "Well, I gave it to her. And she had white rugs on her floor," he added somewhat parenthetically. A breeze put cold hands on the back of our necks. "That was funny," Joe said. He ducked his head, fumbled his zipper clasping together, and rasped the metal runner halfway closed. "Only then I keep on finding out funny things," Joe went on. "You know, like when she said she lost her kid, I thought it died. Only about a month ago, I found out she really lost it. She put it down once, and couldn't find it again, when she was going shopping. And they didn't call the police. Her husband wouldn't let her. I mean what sort of person would be a nut like that. He was a crook, a politician, which is how she got all her money. She's a philanthropist, though, which sort of compensates, huh?"

"I guess so," I said.

"You know, like she's old enough to be my mother," he said, leaning toward me and putting his hand on my shoulder. "That would be something, wouldn't it. I mean if she really was." He scratched his head again. "But I'd sort of like that, really." Then he laughed.

"She's not so bad. It's just her husband sounds like he was awfully crazy. All he did was leave her a lot of money. Which, I guess, was pretty nice."

"It sounds it," I said.

"How did your father die?" Joe asked me, now.

"Fairly well," I said, "everything considered."

"Huh?" Joe asked.

"I think he was very much afraid at first, but then he got used to the idea, only you could tell there were a lot of things he wanted to do, still."

I noticed now that Geo had moved near me and was listening. Loupo walked a little ahead, listening to Margaret and Billy who had gotten into a discussion about birds.

"How did he die?" Geo asked, differently than Joe had.

"Huh?" I said.

"Who was there, what happened. What did you do, what did they do."

"My father was there," I said, "in an oxygen tent. There were too many people there, and I wasn't there long enough. He died, they mourned, and I took my shoes off and walked in the rain by the river and tried to cry."

We reached the Square, now. Buildings opened up and we emptied out under autumn trees.

"Hey look, the fountain," Loupo said, pointing. The circular rim lay on the stone field, among bare trees, before the Arch of Triumph. "They call that the concrete diaphragm."

We laughed.

Coming toward it, tree shifted by darker tree, and the eight stone balustrades that octagonized its edges rotated by us. "There's something in this that reminds me of Silem," Geo said. "Death and a turning stone circle. She could probably improvise a very fine elegy for you."

I was not sure what he was talking about. But he seemed to be talking to me. Loupo had gone ahead now. "Is your mother like she used to be?" Geo asked me.

"I don't know."

"They keep on saying that you have no pain," Geo said. "That's blank verse."

"They said that about him," I said. "That there wasn't any pain."

"Yeah," said Geo.

"I tried to write him a letter the night before he died. But I couldn't do it. I couldn't do it, Geo."

"I wish you and your sister could see yourselves," Geo said.

"Huh?" I asked.

"You make very impressive mourners."

"What's that supposed to mean?"

"I shouldn't have said that, because first it sounds cynical, and second you probably wouldn't understand, anyway."

"Explain," I said.

"There gets a certain stage where action becomes completely mechanical, flows without motivation. Or seems to, is reduced completely to the expiation of some sort of guilt. Why does your sister decide to walk us through a flaming field, why do you suddenly run after her? Nobody gives a reason, nobody objects. But when I conjecture, I get frightened. I'm too fond of you two not to get frightened. Sometimes, though, you become nothing more than a mirror. And that's bad."

"I don't understand," I said.

"I know. Look, what I mean is that I think something very terrible is going to happen to you and if you don't start finding out what is happening to you and what you're letting happen to you, and why. It's what I said before, back on the bridge. It's just that your father's dying isn't going to help."

"I wish I knew what the hell you were talking about," I said.

"You should have an elegy," Geo said.

"I tried," I said. "I couldn't write him though."

"I know," said Geo. He looked at the ground as we walked now. Then he looked up with a sort of questioning expression, and said, "They told me you were not in any pain,

or anything, father. What strange orders,
then, place me here? In the September rain
the inner bastions of my crumbled heart
are flooded through with cold water.
I want these chambers washed in aseptic
quicksilver, luminous, and grave . . ."

He paused for a moment, looked down again, and then went on.

"— I start
at the sound of heels on the pavement. Click-
click-click. I press my bare feet hard against
the stone at the foot of the park stair.
The unknowing man who passes me pulls
me from behind my eyes. Night, draped on air
covers him now. And he's not my father.
And he is not my . . . and the word blinks out
(The uneven cement is wet) and in
the vacuum of the absent, there
in the dark hollow of my convoluted
ear, rife with indistinct whispers, I
hear all the words you could not say.
And sitting here, after the end of day,
I think and keep on thinking, "How inane
I cannot weep a tenth as much as rain."
And I let my head drop on my knee
and crooked forearm; now all I can see
is a stretch of wet cement, my bare foot
on the ground. I cannot choose which:
the wide, wild, ululant coronachs of
home, or my choicely cadenced hysterics,

a strangeness of pre-mourning which to me
means nothing. And that is why, now, I put
my penitent self, barefoot in the night
to ponder all the thoughts you will not leave.
It is my absent grief for which I grieve.
I am silent, father, with the entombed
passions of my mother. Grieve, grave, grieven.
God: the pavement is so wet and so uneven.
And my words are too old, wanting pity
and archaic awe; they will not fill with light.
O, this gray stone city under the night
in which you have no name, they say. The rain
is gray, even in the dull-washed street light.
Mother, a stone under spilled quicksilver,
would have you think the water in my heart is tears.
Though you are so within me now with love, I
find it ludicrous I cannot even cry,
except a little. And all the pulsing fears
are ludicrous again. What must I do?
I will not see the ox, the white lamb
as bone, meat, dung, nor also you.
Christ, order, or compassion, here I am.
They keep on saying that you have no pain.
But through the dim and seeming cellophane
of the oxygen tent that holds your flickering
death, all left bent, we see each other's drowned eyes.
I listen to your inarticulate breath.
And when the blown mind escapes the body's cage,
still the wildness trapped inside will rage
round in the emptiness. So cold, so cold

this night. And all my aging youth, already old."

"O.K.," I said, as quietly as I could. "What am I supposed to do now?" The group's pace had slowed, and turned down the lit alley of McDougal Street.

"I wasn't sure I could still do that," Geo said. "I haven't in a long time. What are you supposed to do?" he laughed a little. "Nothing, I guess."

We moved into the net of muted color beneath the night stitched tight between buildings. Tourists, characters, green woolen sweaters, black silk blouses, flared in a sort of raucous brilliance. "You know," Helen was saying to Daniele, "they shouldn't turn the fountain off at night. They should leave it on, and it would look great, a big sparkle of water under the lights."

"You'd go swimming in it," Daniele said.

"That would be fun; wash some of this soot off. Whose idea was it to go through all those ashes?"

"I ain't sooty," Oona said, looking at his big Michelangelo hands. "I guess you had some of that soot on your before you came."

"I love you too, beautiful," Helen said.

"Hey," Joe said to me, looking at the green bundle of silk. "I guess I better give this back to your sister." He went up to my sister and handed it to her. "I think you dropped this."

"Oh," Margaret said. "Thanks." She was still talking with, or rather listening to Billy. Suddenly she took the scarf, reached up, and tied it around Billy's neck. Billy stopped talking, looked down at the green necklace, flapped his hand to his shoulders and asked, "For me?"

"For you," Margaret said.

Billy shrugged: "Oh." Then he flung his arms out to the side, and let them fall. "Anyway," he continued, "I said, what in the world do I want with a parakeet. But he was very sweet and insistent, so I had a blue parakeet on my hand, or in my cage anyway. For days. And I had to carry water in a little bitty bowl all the way from the bathroom to the bird cage, for days and days. Then, one day, he walked in with a white cockatrice. He said I could give him back the parakeet but would I take care of his cockatrice for him. The cockatrice's name was Hilda. Fine, I carted birdseed for that potential feather duster for two weeks. Then he showed up with two falcons, and a Baltimore oriole. I'm such a good bird keeper, would I please take care of his homeless falcons. Yes, he had cages for them out in the car. My dear, falcons don't eat bird seed. They eat chopped meat. And fingers. I'm expecting him to show up with a partridge in a pear tree any day now. Suppose he brings an eagle. What am I going to do with it? I'm not going to spend the rest of my life with an albatross around my neck. But what can I do, after all *that*, I can't very well tell him to just go away. I guess it's sort of my fault. But he's going to bring an eagle, next. I just know. Someday one of these birds is going to fly off with me. Just fly off." He flapped his arms.

We laughed, and Billy shook the night full of his pale hair. We were walking quickly, overtaking people, passing around them, and shutting up on the other side. We overtook one couple, elderly, who had come down to see the sights. (You could tell.) Loupo was walking behind the man, and suddenly he began to kick the man's heels. The man sort of stumbled two steps, stepped to the side and looked back. “Oh,” he said. “Pardon me.”

“Yeah, sure,” said Loupo. “Pardon shit.” He gave the man a shove.

“Hey look,” the man said.

“Beautiful, baby,” Loupo called. And Oona loomed behind him, closed his hands into fists, and cracked them together. There was a second of silence, and then the woman he was with tugged at his sleeve and looked worried. Suddenly they turned away and fell off into the night. Loupo was laughing. “Hey Daniele,” he cackled. “You think she was a dyke?” pointing after them. “She looked like a dyke to me. You don’t fuck around with them dykes, hear me?”

“Cut it out,” Daniele said.

Loupo grabbed her shoulder and half hissed, “You want me to fuck your ass?”

Suddenly Paul, who had been silent, flung his hand hard and snapping against the back of Loupo’s head. Loupo jumped forward. “Lay off,” said Paul.

“God damn,” howled Loupo. “Cut that shit out.” He turned to Geo. “Tell your sadist friend to cut out the shit.”

People turned to watch us.

“I’ll cut your balls off,” Paul said.

“Fuck you, baby,” said Loupo. Then he looked around, saw the people, and laughed. We continued down the street.

Without particular motivation, we turned down Minetta Alley. By the door of a coffee shop, a girl was sitting on a guitar case and plucking alternate arpeggios of tonic and super tonic, dominant and super dominant. When we gathered around her, she looked up and seemed embarrassed. She was a tall girl;

her hair was long and hung loose over one shoulder. Her face was long and the nose was sharp and shadowed, as her eye sockets were, as the line of her jaw. On the awning, beneath which she sat, there was a spotlight that pointed against a sign on the window which sported a list of phenomenally priced coffees and teas.

"Hey you, sing something," Loupo said.

She laughed and shrugged.

"Come on," he said.

"Keep quiet," Paul said.

She ran the chords once again, shifted her shoulders. Then the guitar chording changed, loudened, and took on measure and accent, honed itself to a double bell note, a low and high string together. "This is a song about a silky," she said. "That's a beast that's a man on the land and a thing like a seal in the water. He has a child by the girl this song's about." And the belling of the chord rose again, and her voice, suddenly like a bright pane of glass, spread under it,

"An earthly nouris . . ."

and the chord suddenly dropped a whole tone,

"and aye she sings . . ."

and it dropped again,

". . . ba lilly ween, sayin' . . ."

and an opening into the dominant, the full chord opening into dominant, rolling major in the low strings,

". . . where shall I my bairn's father,
far less . . ."

and at the beat it contracted into minor,

". . . the land that he steps in."

Her fine little finger hammered on a modal fifth, whitening the chord, paling it into a skeletal ghost of itself.

"Then ane arose to her bed fit
and a grumily guest, I'm sure was he,
sayin' . . ."

and the verse opened again, major under the rising soprano transparency of her voice,

". . . here I am, they bairn's father,
Although I be not comily." and the minor rumbling bleached into the hollow modal chord.

"I am a man upon the land,
and I'm a silky in the sea,
and when I'm far and far fra' land,
my dwelling is in Shule Skeree."

She lifted her head now, and her voice fixed the air, poiniarded the evening, white-moth like to the song.

"And he ha' ta'en a purse of go'd,
and he ha' put it on her knee, sayin'
gi' to me my little young son
and take thee up thy nouris fee."

Thunder entered in the low strings, now, and, her neck high, the voice covered itself, mounting on its own power:

"And it shall pass on a summer's day,
when the sun . . ."

at each beat, now, her fingers flipped hard across the strings,

". . . shines hot . . ."

and they flipped and cut clean through the arpeggio

". . . on every stane,

that I

shall take,

my little

young son,"

and the voice evened into the contractive minor, ominous now, dark and full of shadow:

"And teach him for to swim his lane."

and the modal glared like a hollow white bone, shifted to minor, then broke out again. The voice shifted from transparency to the sheen of steel:

"And you shall marry a proud gunnér,
and a very proud gunnér I'm sure he'll be,
and the very first *shot* . . ."

and I thought the strings had snapped, because there was silence, but then the voice heaved on,

". . . that e'er he shoots . . ."

and there was silence once more; and once more the rhythm reared swell from swell, almost over the voice now,

"He'll shoot both my young son and me."

Modal, minor, modal, minor:

"I am a man upon the land,"

She sang, her voice diminishing to transparency, and the chording following her down in volume,

". . . and I'm silky in the sea,"

and click of her nails could be heard on the strings, now:

"... and when I'm far and far fra' land,
My dwelling is in Shule Skeree."

And the chord broke, retarded, and ended.

Other people had come up too.

Then someone large was pushing through us. "O.K. break it up." A policeman, large and dark blue, erupted into the crowd. "Hey, lady, you can't sing on the street. This is a public place and you're blocking traffic. Come on, god damn it, break it up now."

"Let her sing," someone called.

The girl had gotten up from her guitar case and was holding her instrument by the neck.

"Break it up," the cop said again, and shoved out from both sides of him.

"Fuck you, flat foot," Loupo said. "Don't push." Then I saw him send a small, sharp elbow into the policeman's blue flank. All I know is that was how it started. The policeman probably fell back and stepped on someone else and got pushed again. And once Oona gave him a shove forward and he landed against the awning pole of the coffee shop while other people surged around him. The awning shook, and the spotlight against the shop sign suddenly swung free and washed a bright beam through us like a white knife. The ratchet must have caught because three quarters of the way through its arc, it stopped, the beam fixed suddenly on Billy, pale haired, pale face, the green noosed on his neck. Under the light his face flew open and he screamed. "Oh my God. Oh my dear God. Now we've done it."

In the crowd, the girl cried, "My guitar!" (Someone pushed me in the back, before I saw the instrument, still unharmed, raise on high hands above the crowd . . .) The guitar came for me, and I saw that Geo was carrying it. "Come on," he said.

We got around the corner fast. Margaret was already there. "Well, there you are."

Loupo sprinted around after us. "Hey," he laughed. "Did we do all that?"

"Why don't you keep out of trouble," Geo said.

"No fun," shrugged Loupo.

Next came Billy, rubbing his head and staggering a little; Helen, Paul, Oona; and then Daniele, pulling the arm of the girl who had been singing.

The girl looked bewildered and was pulling back.

"There's your guitar," Daniele said, pointing to Geo. "I told you I knew who had it."

"Oh," the girl said. "Thank you." The black case banged across her shin as she walked.

"We better get out of here quickly," Geo said. "All we have to do is wait for that thing to come around the corner."

Then there was a siren blowing somewhere.

"Here we go," Geo said, walking quickly. And we all started after him. The girl finished putting her guitar in her case and came too. We flowered up from the scuffle, now, passing through descending groups of people like meshing tines, and then we were laughing and going slowly again. "Hey," Loupo said to the girl. "You sing well."

The girl smiled and said, "Thanks."

"You should do that professionally. I bet if it wasn't for that fuzz fucker you'd a' gotten money."

"I do sing professionally," the girl said. "At least some times."

"Oh," Loupo said.

"I've seen you," Geo said. "You sing in the Village some times."

"Yes," the girl said. "You do too, don't you?"

"I have," Geo said.

"You sing?" I asked Geo. "I never knew that."

"You knew I played the guitar."

"I never heard you."

"You will, someday," Geo said.

"I liked that song," Daniele said. "Where does it come from?"

"It's Welsh," the girl said. "The words I got out of the Oxford Book of Ballads. The tune was made up by a girl at Oberlin."

"What's your name?" Daniele asked.

"Ann," the girl said.

"My name is Daniele," Daniele introduced herself. "I really liked that. Do you go to Oberlin?"

"Not now. I'm taking a year off."

"You too?" asked Geo.

"I have a brother at college," Helen said. "I wish he'd come home and get my mother off my back."

"Is he at Oberlin?" Ann asked.

"No. At least I think he's still at school. He's sort of wild, and I'm not really sure where he is. For about two months we thought he was dead. Only we got a postcard from him. My mother gets very upset about him. She wants him back and she doesn't want him back. Sometimes I think she's afraid of him, really."

"Why?" Ann asked.

Suddenly Billy interrupted, "Hey, you know this thing looks pretty silly on me," and he was untying my sister's scarf. "Green is definitely not my color." He suddenly leaned over and gave my sister a peck on the cheek. "Thank you my dear, but green isn't my color."

Then he whirled around and jammed the scarf in Helen's mouth. "You may wear it a little while. It looks better on you."

Helen took the scarf out of her mouth, punched her hips with both fists, and said, "Hey, what the hell is the matter with you?"

"Nothing," said Billy. Then he began to giggle hysterically and pranced off ahead of us.

"God damn," said Helen. "I think he's crazy."

"What were you saying about your brother?" Ann asked.

"Huh? Just that I'm waiting for him to get back. I've got a stepfather see, and he's kind of funny sometimes. My real father was a solider. When he came home, back in 1945, he had a medal and everybody thought he was very brave. Two days later he fell down in the bathtub and fractured his skull. So my mother got married again, and the guy I got for a stepfather is a louse. But my mother's worse. So I'm waiting."

"He must be at summer school, now," Ann said.

"He's away all the time," Helen said. "He doesn't like home very much, and I can understand why, too. Hey, Margaret," she suddenly called. "You want your scarf back?"

Silently my sister took it from her, and then fell in beside me.

"Where do we go now?" Loupo asked. "Anybody got any ideas?"

"I'm going to have to leave you soon," Ann said. "I've got to go to a friend's house. That's where I was about to go when you came along. It was nice meeting you though."

"Hey, is it a party?" said Loupo. "We'll all go."

"Well," said Ann hesitantly, "it's sort of a party, but I can't bring a whole group of strangers in."

"Come on," said Loupo. "Why not? I want to go to a party."

"Lay off," said Geo. "Sort of ignore him," he told her.

"God damn," said Loupo. "I haven't been to a party in a long time."

"I'm sorry," Ann started.

"I wanna go to a party," Loupo said. "Anybody know of a good party on tonight?" Loupo got another skull-whack from Paul. So he shut up, I guess.

Suddenly Geo stopped. "Oh," he said.

"What is it?" Daniele asked.

"I think I know where my wife is," said Geo.

"Where," Daniele asked.

Geo reached in his back pocket and pulled out a sheaf of crumbled envelopes, and looked at them. "Yes," he said. "I was supposed to mail these about three days ago."

"What are they?" Daniele asked.

"Well," said Geo. "One is for you," he handed Daniele an envelope, "One is for you," and he handed Paul one, "and this one is for you and Margaret." I took the last, and opened it.

Dear Jimmy and Margaret,

I hope this will not be an inconvenience, but could we please postpone our dinner until next Wednesday, the twenty-third. Something has come up that will occupy Geo and myself, but we will look forward to seeing you in a week. Thank you so much,

Laile.

I looked up at Geo. “Well,” I said. “What happened?”

“I donno,” said Geo. “This is silly. We got invited to some party by one of Laile’s friends. I didn’t particularly want to go, and I didn’t think she did. When she got the invitation, she said something about postponing you people, and later she gave me these to mail. And I completely forgot. I guess she went on to the party.”

Daniele *humphed.* “Some people,” she said. “Well, where the hell is it. You probably better get there before she leaves and really gets mad at you.”

“She never mentioned it to me except that once. Didn’t say a thing. It completely slipped my mind.”

“Do you remember where the party was?” Daniele asked, practically.

“Yeah,” said Geo. He looked at us all, now. “You know, I’m awfully sorry.”

“Don’t be sorry,” Daniele said. “Just get over there.”

“What about yours?” Loupo asked. “Can we go to your party, man?”

“Sorry,” Geo said. “Not this one either.”

"Shit," Loupo said. We were walking up the street slowly again. Suddenly Loupo perked up. "Hey, let's all go in there." He pointed across the street to a glass windowed café.

"Why?" Oona's big, truck-motor voice asked.

"They got good jazz in there," Loupo said. "No party, O.K. Maybe we can hear some good jazz."

"Does it cost money?" Joe asked. "I can't go."

"Naw," said Loupo. "Come on. Just for a minute, Geo, you too, just see what it sounds like." He started across the street, and we followed.

"You should go on to the party," Daniele said to Geo.

"Ten minutes more won't hurt," Geo said.

The place was dark, and thick with alcohol smells. We bunched into the vestibule of the place. Over the heads of people at tables, the little platform was crowded with musicians, the drummer in front; trumpet, saxophone, and bass fiddle squeezed in behind. As we went in, the lights on the musicians suddenly went red, and the music increased in volume and tempo, the brass glare of the horns, the sea thud of the bass losing themselves behind the rattling of the drum skins, and the *boom, boom, boom* of the bass drum, hammered with the foot pedal again and again. A clap of sound, and the lights went blue, and the silences except the sticks on the cymbals. The brass disk tilted from us beneath it, rivets hissed into an octagon of blue stars. The trumpet began to bleat above it, a high note, brilliant light tinkle, and then it dropped down, and began a melody.

I glanced aside once and saw in the shadowed vestibule that Loupo, standing behind Joe, had locked his arms around Joe's belly and was resting his chin on the boy's shoulder. So close like that they looked sort of weird. But Joe didn't seem to mind. The melody turned like a bright dancer, turned like silver chord on velvet. Somebody was coming through the tables toward us. I really didn't see him until he was saying, "You'll have to sit down and order something or leave."

"Come on," said Loupo. "Let's get out of here." We hobbled around in the crowded space and got back onto the cool street.

"Bad jazz is annoying," Paul said.

"Was that bad?" I asked him.

"Well, it wasn't good."

"What do you know about jazz?"

"I play the drums," Paul told me. "And that was bad jazz. They don't have to light good jazz up with red and blue spot lights."

"Where's Ann?" Daniele asked.

"I think she took the opportunity to get the hell away from you bunch of nuts," Helen said, looking up and down the street.

"Christ," said Loupo, "everybody's cutting out. What a dead evening. Bad jazz depresses me. Hey, come on, let's cut out of here," and suddenly he was running up the street. First Joe, and then the rest like panthers streaked after him, leaving Margaret, myself, Geo and Daniele standing in the street.

"Well, that's enough of them for one evening."

"I wonder who has my scarf?" Margaret said.

"You didn't get it back?" I asked.

"Nope," she laughed.

"Where is this party you're going to? Daniele asked.

Geo said a name and an address.

"Oh," said Daniele. "Her." Then she looked up the street, "Maybe I better follow them, just to make sure they don't kill somebody." She turned to Margaret and me. "Nice to meet you," she smiled. "So long, Geo. Thanks for dinner."

Then she started quickly up the street after the others, calling back, "Say hello to Laile for me."

"Well," said Geo, after a moment. "What do you think of them?"

"You have strange friends," Margaret said.

"Sometimes they're the only bearable ones," said Geo. "You know, they're mixed up so much in their own problems that they don't have time to get mixed up in yours. That can be refreshing after a while."

"I guess so," Margaret said. "Some of them are cute."

Geo laughed. "You two," he said, "are perfectly welcome to come along to this thing with me. I just couldn't walk in with all of them though. It's a very informal kind of thing, but not that informal."

"What sort of a party is it?" I asked.

"The girl who's giving it fancies herself the holder of great salons. You can meet all sorts of minor lights there. Like me. Or Edna Silem, or the steady contributors to the little magazines. Come on; Laile does want to meet you and it might as well be tonight as next week. You want to come?"

"Well, if it's informal enough for you to come in blue-jeans and a flannel shirt, I guess we can get by," said Margaret. "Sure."

2.

The apartment in which we landed was large, furnished with lots of scrolled brass and warm carved wood, and crowded. The hostess, in a blue dress that looked like it was covered with sky colored shaving foam, flung her arms around Geo and said, "There you are! You've brought friends. Lovely. Where did you leave your wife?"

"If you'll get your paws off of me for a few minutes, I can probably extricate her from that snake pit in your living room," he said, pointing over her shoulder.

The hostess giggled, and embraced him once more.

"Get off, will you?" Geo said. "I've got lice." Undaunted, the hostess caught him by the hand and started to lead him off into the living room. Geo looked back over his shoulder and called, "Look, we'll reconnoiter again in half an hour under the Picasso."

Margaret and I laughed, and went in after him. We were whirled apart, and I found myself meandering past clots of conversation, arguments, dirty stories, and at last bumped into a table on which there were drink makings. I mixed something together in a large glass that was mostly bubbles and finally swiped a seat from a departing middle aged lady with a large wreath of fake lilies on her head. Like moths, a gray cloud of pale young men fluttered after her, so I could spread out.

Suddenly someone jammed his big hand in between me and what I was drinking and said, "Well, there you are. I was wondering when you'd get here."

I shook the hand, moved it someplace else, and looked at the owner, who looked at me, and didn't recognize me. "Oh," he said. "I don't know you. I thought you were . . ." Then he shrugged and sat down. After a moment, he said, "My name is O'Donnels," and the hand flopped up to be shaken like a pudgy pink fish.

I shook it again, and said, "My name is Jimmy Calvin. Pleased to meet you."

"Same. You don't come to . . ." and he intoned the hostess' name ". . . little to-do's much, do you. This is the first time I've seen you here in a long time."

"This is the first time you've seen me here at all," I said.

"You're a newcomer then." Suddenly he pointed across the room. "Do you know who that is?"

Geo, one hand shoved in the back of his jeans pocket, a glass in the other was expounding something very heatedly to a bunch of people, bouncing up and down as though he was impatient to get to the bathroom.

"That's Geo Keller," said O'Donnels. "You know who he is."

"Oh," I said. "Who is he?"

"Well, he wrote that obscene poem that raised such a cloud, remember?"

"Oh yes," I said.

"He comes here a lot of times. Edna Silem too. But she's not here tonight."

"Who's Edna Silem?" I asked.

"Oh, haven't you read her book? Or are you one of those people who doesn't like poetry?"

"I'm afraid I'm out of it," I said.

"Her stuff is simply unbelievable," O'Donnels went on. "But of course she's older than he is, and doesn't go in for the same sort of notoriety. There are some people, and you'll run into both kinds this evening, who'll praise her stuff all over Keller's there. Others who think she's too fragile and think he's just great. The people who like her, though, think Kellar's coarse and slightly prosy, but I think they both have something. But whatever you say about him, he's a brilliant young man. I was here once when both of them were here, together, and they sat down and talked in couplets for half an hour."

"They what?" I said.

"Had the whole place listening. This was a couple of years ago. I don't think Keller was even twenty."

"What did they do that for?"

"Oh, it was just for fun. But he's smart, knows his stuff. This beat stuff is through; you look at them for the new poetry."

"What do you think of his poems?" I asked.

"Well, what I've read," he said. And he didn't seem to think the sentence needed finishing. "You see, the difference between him and Selim is that she travels only on the strength of her poetry, while he enjoys dirt and scandal."

"Oh?" I asked.

"You know about his play, don't you?"

"I don't know he had written one."

"Well, I suppose he would like to forget it. You'd think he'd have had sense enough not to have written it, and if he had written it, not to get it performed."

"Tell me about it?" I asked, looking off again at Geo.

"Well, dear Mr. Keller, during his bright, prolific and notorious youth was taken under the wing of an ex-novelist, ex-publisher, ex-literary light who knew just about everybody there was to know and who was still on speaking terms with them, no less. Which was good for Mr. Keller. He was a man named Sloan, that had invited Keller to spend some time with him, on the strength of some of his manuscripts. After all sorts of things, when Keller had gotten a little notice, or more notoriety, over that obscene thing, he came out with a play based on the life of Rimbaud. Well, there had been rumors of some sort of unpleasant break up between Sloan and Keller, and something violent. So when this play came up, with this particular subject, everybody began looking for hints of what had happened between Sloan and Keller. And there are hints all over it. It was done briefly off-Broadway, where it lasted about three months. But because of the nasty things some people were saying, they took it off."

"I didn't even know that he'd written a play."

"Oh, he's written all sorts of things. The manuscripts get circulated around, and this is where to come if you want a chance to read them."

"Really?" I said. "How was the play?"

"How would a play by any nineteen-year-old author about Rimbaud be? Pretentious. But entertaining."

"Oh."

"But that was two years ago. I hear his work is maturing a lot, thought I haven't read his most recent stuff."

"Oh," I said again.

"And marriage will probably be good for him."

"What time is it?" I asked.

"Nearly ten thirty," O'Donells said, looking at his watch. I looked as if I had something to do, and got up and went into a corner with my glass of mostly ginger ale, and stood there with my eyes closed.

"Hey," someone said.

I opened my eyes and it was my sister.

"You asleep?"

"Almost."

"Nutty bunch of people," she went on. She was holding a glass of something amber up under her chin with both hands. "I've met two people so far and all they can talk about is Geo."

"You too?" I asked. "You want to compare notes?"

"Not particularly. I told one girl that I'd come to the party with him; she asked me what I knew about his wife. I told her I didn't know her very well, and I'm sure from the look in her face she'll have me his mistress in about ten minutes."

"Did you know he'd written a play?"

"No," said Margaret, sipping.

"Someone told me about it."

Margaret nodded. "I'm going to go look for the Picasso," she said.

"I'll meet you there in a few minutes."

"I don't think he's found his wife," Margaret said, before she went away.

From where I was standing I couldn't see Geo. I leaned away from the wall and zigged one way and zagged another till I was near the door. Suddenly Geo was at my elbow, "Where are you going?"

"Does this place have a roof? I think I want some air."

"Good idea. Laile's not here, and I can't find anybody that's said they've seen her."

The door closed behind us. "It's hot in there," I said.

"Shall I go back in and get Margaret?" Geo asked.

"If she wants some air, she'll come out. We'll just be a few minutes."

Geo shrugged and walked along beside me. We mounted iron banistered stairs, turned again, and mounted another flight. The building was tall and we were on the lower floors. Once I looked up through the diminishing rectangles of the stair-well. The top ones faded into black. "You know what this reminds me of?" I said, looking back at Geo.

"No, what?"

"At church, the day we climbed up to hear the bells."

"Yeah," said Geo, and he grinned.

"Only things have changed a lot, I guess."

"I'm older, you're older," said Geo.

"You've written plays, poems."

"I'd written poems when we climbed the tower before," said Geo. "I think I'd even tried a play."

"My father is dead; he was alive before."

"I guess with you that does make a difference," Geo said.

"I didn't know you had a play produced," I told him.

"Who, me? What play?"

"A play about Rimbaud?"

"Oh," said Geo. "That. It wasn't exactly a play. It was something I wrote more for a joke than anything else. Three friends of mine did it about a year ago."

"Two years ago," I said.

"Yeah, I guess. Almost. They did it in one of the coffee shops in the Village. It only had three characters and it acts well in a small place. It was fun. Ran for almost two months."

"Three."

"Three? No, I don't think so." He picked at his nose with his little finger. "Who told you about it?"

"Somebody named O'Daniels."

Geo frowned for a moment. "I don't think I know him."

"Can I read it?"

"I probably have a copy of it someplace around the house. Sure, if I can find it." We reached the roof door, and walked out onto the cindered plane. The night was murky with the red wash from traffic lamps below.

"Incidentally," I said, "thank you for the poem for my father." We reached the roof edge; below, Central Park, scarred with light, stretched in a gnarled miniature troll garden.

"A lot of it was written before for another poem."

"Oh?" I said. "Well, thanks anyway. Can you really improvise blank verse like that?"

"It can be done; it isn't very hard," Geo said. "Admittedly though, it's seldom very good." He paused. "It has a tendency to be sing-song. But simply get the rhythm in your head, and you can spout the silly stuff for hours."

We laughed.

I stretched out over the street, till I could see the building face, the perpendicular lines arrowing together toward the pavement. "I don't usually like high places," I said. "It's not that I'm afraid of falling. I'm always afraid maybe I'll just decide to jump. Out of curiosity, you know?"

There were a half a dozen people milling in the street in front of the building, making little L's with their own shadows, almost the size of printing letters. I thought of a lot of glass.

Glass pavement, glass air, I hovered above the glass, Japanese miniature trees. Little toy glass light bulbs in the street lamps, and it wasn't very far away. Glass, glass, or painted on glass; the small people were twists of wire moving under glass, and the whole thing would break with the ring of glass bells, snapped quartz, the reverberation of a crystal bell. Thick paint, green, brown, but mostly dark blue, dribbling down the other side of glass. Or water, thin water, clear and tasting salty.

I could put my hand out, push it, and the pieces would turn and then close over my hand, and I would be looking at my arm severed and behind glass. Then Geo took my wrist and very firmly pulled me back from the balustrade, and as my face came back, the city and its jeweled skyline dropped below me quickly.

"Are you that unsure of yourself?" asked Geo.

"Huh?" I said, not remembering what I'd spoken before. When I did, after a second of looking into his dark, puzzled face, I said, "Oh. Yeah. Maybe."

"Let's go down and get Margaret," he said.

We walked back to the door, and entered into the door, a frame passing back across the smoky bowl of sky into the dull safety of artificial light.

3.

Margaret was waiting near a bad print of *Dancers Resting.* We all got to the door, dived past the hostess who was diving after Geo, and walked the few flights down into the street-lobby.

"Hi," Loupo said. He was sitting cross legged on a red leather bench beside a white marble nude. "Find Laile?"

"What are you doing here?" Geo said.

Daniele, who was just coming in the large glass door, said, "Uh-oh. Geo, I'm sorry. He wormed it out of me. They'd all decided to go someplace else, and then he asked me where the party was, and, like an ass, I told him. So he ducks off after you."

"That's all right," Geo said.

"I want to go to a party," Loupo said.

"No," said Geo.

"Where's Laile?" Daniele asked.

Geo shrugged. "She wasn't there."

"Oh," said Daniele. We started outside.

"Can't we go upstairs for a few minutes?" asked Loupo.

We ignored him and went on to the street. The entire mob of them had gathered in front of the building — the people I had seen from the roof.

"Hey," said Margaret, when she recognized them. "Does anybody have my scarf?"

"You mean this?" big Oona stepped forward, and drew the green scarf from his jacket pocket. "Someone dropped it so I picked it up." He extended the Gordian knot of his fist.

"No, that's all right," Margaret said. "You can hold it for me. I just wanted to know who had it."

We started up along the edge of the park. Joe fell in beside me again, "What sort of party was it?"

"Crowded and noisy," I said. "And hot. We didn't stay long."

"Yeah," said Joe, jingling his buckles as he zipped his jacket. It was getting chilly.

"You wanna go hear some really good music?" Paul asked.

"Sure," Loupo said. "Where?"

"I can't stay up too late," Oona said. "I gotta get up tomorrow."

"What for?" asked Paul.

"Gotta work," said Oona.

"You work?" asked Paul. "I didn't know that. Where?"

"Some guy who owns a stable down below the park here. He rents horses out to ride in the park."

"What do you do?"

"Shovel horse shit," Oona said. "At least tomorrow. I gotta clean out the whole place. That's gonna be fun. You know what I think I'll do; instead of shoveling all day, I'll just turn the fire hose on it, and wash all the stuff out, if the guy isn't around to watch."

"Sounds like fun," Paul said.

We turned away from the park, now, off on a side street. "Where are you taking us?" Geo asked.

"You'll see," Paul said.

We turned again, going up the avenue now. The streets cramped in on themselves. The building faces rose like burned rock, broken and pitted, crumbled cornices, fire escapes aslant. The air chilled.

"It smells damp," said Helen.

"The river's not too far away," Paul said.

The place we ended up that night, near twelve, was at a little, broken, red brick church. Stained glass windows on the church's side slipped patch and blotch of red and yellow light across first Paul's face, then Helen's, Margaret's , Billy's, Daniele's and Loupos's, as we went toward the door.

"What's this? Daniele asked.

We entered the wooden door and crowded into the vestibule. At the opening of the door, there was a voice high under the vaulted ceiling, dark, and saying:

". . . . Ponder these words. Ponder, Children! 'The end of all flesh is come before me; for the earth is filled with violence through them; and behold, I will destroy them with the earth,' and wasn't it said, so, here in the book? You have seen, Children. Daughters, you have seen it in the streets of the city. My sons, you have seen in the faces of both Ham and Lazarus. Sodom burned, and she that looked back became salt. Where are Nineveh and Babylon? Hagar nursed Ishmael by a fountain in the desert. John baptized His body in the Jordan; Moses broke open the sea. But when God said: 'The end of all flesh is come before me . . .' Then all the oceans become one ocean and there was no land. No land, no land."

The tiles of the floor were dirty and cracked. The lamps from the beamed ceiling gave dim yellow light, rich with the wood. There were mostly women in the pews. Behind the iron railed pulpit were wooden choir benches and choir rails. The seated singers numbered maybe ten. Even from here you could see their robes were worn and frayed at the sleeves.

The preacher coughed, ran his finger around the neck of his surplice, and came down the steps of the pulpit. The choir stood up, now, and a man and three women stepped forward on the altar porch. From somewhere an electric organ started to play: two high notes were broken and wheezed a continual shrill dissonance.

One of the women, gaunt like an abraded mahogany scarecrow, stepped forward. She took a breath, her hands jumped together like twined claws, and a voice, like something that had spent most of its life under high ceilings, in great caves or in the reverberating corridors of cathedrals, leapt up like a bell clapper in the small building.

"Set free my soul,"

she sang, the voice sang, going down and ending on a Bach-like ornamentation.

"Let me cross your dark sea,"

and on the last note, taking advantage of the flat vowel, she soared up into range of small bells, and crying, and then came down like water over rocks, again, and again, almost crying. She heaved in a breath at the end and sang:

"And let me go home,"

dropping to a lowness that rivaled the organ; her head went down on her chest and the note got nearly lost.

"Home, my Lord, to thee."

The choir stood up now, and the men and two women behind her began to sing and rock back and forth.

"Set free . . ."

the woman sang, and like stones flung on brass cymbals, the three behind her shouted in chord[166]: "Set free . . ."

"My soul . . ."

sang the woman, and they sang:

"My soul . . ."

"Let me cross . . ."

"I wanna cross . . ."

"Your dark sea . . ."

"The dark sea . . ."

"And let . . ."

"Why don't you let . . ."

". . . me go home . . ."

"Let me go home."

and they meshed now, beating consonants against the rooves of their mouths and music against the ceiling,

"Home, my Lord, to thee."

And then again, this time with the choir, and the lead voice, now broke into a ululant obbligato above,

"Why don't you let, Oh God, Oh Lord why don't you let me cross your terrible and stormy sea.

For don't you know, I don't want to be crucified," cried the lead singer once more, cracking the soprano continuo like rock on glass.

"Go home, my Lord, to thee."

and on the last note the lead singer soared all the way up in a sort of super acciaccatura three octaves away from where she'd started.

---

[166] Likely this was supposed to have been "shouted a chord."

"Why don't you set free my soul,"

the chorus sang, while the trio began again:

"Set free my soul, Let me cross . . ."

". . . your dark and terrible and
stormy sea,"

Came the choir out from under them,

"Let me go . . ."

started the trio, and then the lead singer, the congregation, and the choir against them, erupted,

"Don't you know I don't want to be crucified," and then the many voices became cogs on two meshed circles of sounds,

"Go home, my Lord to thee."

Again the soprano in the chorus bladed the air apart with her high note, ringing like struck steel.

"Set free my soul . . ."

"Will you save me!"

"Let me cross your dark sea . . ."

"Save me! Will you save . . ."

"Oh! My Lord . . ."

"And let me go home . . ."

"Oh yes. I want to go . . ."

"Home, my Lord to thee."

"Let me go home!"

"Set free my soul . . ."

"Please let me go home, Lord."

"Let me cross your dark and terrible and stormy sea."

"So long, so long!"

"For don't you know, I don't want to be crucified . .
"Let me go home and be saved . .
"Go home, my Lord to thee . . ."
"Oh, they hurt my hands, my feet . . ."
"Did you see the Blood."
"Will you save me. Save . . ."
"Set free my soul . . ."
"The sky was white . . ."
"It was black, Lord . . ."
"Let me cross your dark sea . . ."
"Did you see him. Did you see the lamb."
"Oh, Lord, I have been washed.
I have been baptized."
"Let me go home . . ."
"My hands, my feet. The wine, the blood . . . !"
"I don't want to be crucified, Lord."
"Home, my Lord to thee . . ."

A rhythm of sea waves, earthquakes, and hands exhausted sound, and heels snapped down on the floor, arch of sound and architrave taut to snapping, sundered throats. "'Alleluja!" someone shouted, and "'Alleluja," I heard someone say softly.

"Set free my soul,
Let me cross your dark sea.
And let me go home,
Home, my Lord, to thee."

Then the lead singer, over the roll of the organ, sang again, "Home. . . ." and the voice took itself up, down and up and down again through an octave, ". . . my Lord . . ." and lowering over the organ's chords, ". . . to . . ." into deep inverted "Thee . . ." with the trembling of deep hands.

There should have been silence. But the two broken notes of the organ shot the stillness with electronic dissonance. It made my stomach feel uncomfortable. I glanced around and saw that Loupo was going out the door already. I should have stayed to see if there was going to be any more. But Paul, and then Geo followed him quickly. The rest of us came too.

Loupo was halfway across the street ahead of us. A damp breeze cooled my face and, ahead of me, flung Loupo's bright blue shirt collar and red hair violently backward. Another song had started now, and I could hear the organ. As the music hewed free of its rhythmic mooring, and the voices began, suddenly Loupo screamed, and went down on his knees in the street. His voice was a scimitar of sound that stopped us all, and then sent us running after him.

But before we reached him, he leaped to his feet and started to flee. At the corner (there were no cars) he tripped and rolled halfway across the street. Oona got there first, and hefted him up like a sack of something dead. Only perpendicular, he started shooting out lots of arms and legs and howling. He whirled loose from the big arms, suddenly, nearly fell, and danced backwards, crouching. He laughed once, flung his hands like claws up across his face, and screamed. And before the scream was finished, he'd whirled, beat those thin sneakered feet against the ground and was halfway down the next street.

We chased him to a subway, down to the stile, where he almost slammed his body in half running into a turnstile. It knocked the wind out of him and he fell down again, holding onto the wooden bar, his head flung forward on his chest.

Paul got him to his feet, and when he turned him around, there were tears all down his face.

"What the hell is the matter with you?" said Oona, panting.

Loupo suddenly straightened up, put his finger to his lips, and hissed: "*Shhhhh.*" Then he looked from one to the other of us, and giggled. He moved like an animal, crouched and hurt.

We followed with the strain despair of the unprotected, not knowing when he would break out again. We followed him into the subway, and at last he got on a train and sat down across from the rest of us quite calmly. Under the car's fluorescent lights we could see the dirt on the knees of his pants and the streaks on his face. The underarms of his blue shirt were dark.

Suddenly, after we had ridden for nearly forty minutes, and relaxation and the late hour had netted my muscles with fatigue, Loupo leapt from his seat and was off out the door and down the platform. We sprinted after him, had to follow him up one spiral metal staircase by an elevator. It was a deep subway station. When we came out into the darkness, the great hill of Ft. Tryon Park bloated beside us up the night. Loupo passed beneath a street light, stopped once, flung his hair back and screamed up at the dark hill, "God damn it you bitch!" and then was off into the darkness again and the choke of his own crying.

"Damn, he's ducked into the park," Geo said, running along beside me. The infrequent lights caught Loupo's form before us, slipping shadows behind and then ahead of him as he passed beneath them. Paul caught him finally, then Oona, followed by the rest of us.

"Good God," said Billy, "I'm sure all this running isn't doing anybody any good." He turned to my sister. "How do you manage in that dress, dear?"

Loupo was panting.

"What is wrong?" Geo finally demanded.

"I'm gonna be saved," whispered Loupo. He broke away now, took two steps forward, but was too tired to keep running.

"What do you mean?" Daniele asked. She had come up to him and taken his shoulder.

Loupo flung an arm forward up the hill. "Don't you see?" he asked. He began walking, and we crowded around him. "We're gonna be saved," he said. "No more trouble, no nothing."

He began to go on like this, his speech through my own weariness taking on the strange logic of the word obbligato that backs a fever dream. It was not until the fourth or fifth back track of the path that we saw suddenly through the trees the flood-lit walls above us on the rocks of the great granite Cloisters. "We'll be saved!" Loupo suddenly howled, and burst forward from us again. Again we ran after him, and came up against the black barred gate that marched across the path. Loupo ran up to it and pressed his face against the bars, holding onto them tight.

"I gotta get in," he said. "I gotta get in there!" The tears were running down his face I saw.

"You can't get in there now," Daniele said. "Come on, you better go home."

"I gotta get in there," Loupo said. "We gotta get in. The Virgin's in there. She'll save us. We'll be saved."

"It's all locked up, Loupo," Daniele said.

“Come on, friend,” Geo said.

“I gotta be saved,” Loupo said, and his voice broke up onto the high disoriented sound of sobbing. “I gotta be saved in the lap of the Virgin.”

4.

We argued with him, softly, and at last he came away, and in a sort of painful exhaustion, at least for me, we dropped down through the night. We got on the subway, and inertia kept us on past stops I knew and stops I didn’t.

Joe, who was sitting next to me again, once asked me, under the rain roar, “Hey, are you Spanish?”

“No,” I said.

“Greek?”

“No,” I said. “Negro.”

I didn’t particularly feel like talking.

“I thought you were Spanish,” he said. “Some niggers look like spics,” then he laughed. “Some spics look like niggers. I’m spic,” he laughed.

“Oh,” I said. I don’t know why I should remember this out of the welling train ride through the sound of tunnels and concrete. As I said before, no one even bothered to get off, and once I leaned over and went to sleep for a little while on Margaret’s shoulder (she was sitting on the other side); but at any rate, we were turned out into the still, dark morning at the City’s end, near the dark, foggy bay, the lights of the ferry terminal reflecting on the wet skin that slicked the streets either from drizzle or the spray of street-cleaning trucks.

5.

Someone, I think it was Joe, suggested we ride across on the ferry and back. Torpidity had flooded us until the slightest active suggestion was followed without analysis.

I remember Geo said to Margaret, "Don't you have to get home eventually?"

"I suppose so," Margaret said. "But I'm not looking forward to it."

And I realized how much my staying out now was because I didn't want to plow through my mother's annoyance at our having gone out at all.

We walked up the steps, paid our nickels, and meandered through the large yellow waiting room and out onto the ramp. The sliding doors rolled back revealing sky just breaking from night, rich with violet finer than dye.

Chill grasped our wrists and necks as we walked around the edge of the boat to the front. Dull fog blew about us as we went forward in the early morning. There were maybe two or three more people on the wet front deck. Geo and I leaned up against the side rail and looked out at the sheeted blue of river and sky. Billy was capering about before Margaret in the midst of another ludicrous tale, when a triad of gulls dropped from the mist.

"Gulls," said Billy. "Oh, my Lord. Seagulls. Well, I guess that's better than falcons."

The motor thrilled deeply, and we lugged forward away from the guide slip of bound pilings. Daniele, also against the rail, turned away now, the wind shaking the sleeves of her jacket, her eyes squinting into the gray haze like lights behind her face. A boy in a leather windbreaker stood away from us; the wind flicked his dark hair. Another bird coalesced in the fog, flapping before us as if trying to stay visible. Then suddenly it fell away to the side and dematerialized in the mist.

"I wonder does the shore come up like that?" I asked.

"I don't know," said Geo. "I've never seen it this foggy before."

I felt compressed, with a familiar tiredness that hurt my stomach. I touched it with my hand. Then I turned away from the rail. Margaret and Billy had gone inside. Loupo had sat down in a corner of the door, put his head down on his arms, and gone to sleep I think. There was a couple embracing at the corner where the railing joined the cabin in the rich fog. Looking, I suddenly realized that the taller form was Daniele, and the shorter one Helen, their faces, their mouths, their opened eyes moving slowly over one another's.

Oona and Paul leaned out over the water, and Joe had gone back inside to get something to eat, he said.

The boy next to Geo in the leather windbreaker, wasn't wearing any shoes, I saw suddenly there was no horizon. Sky and water blended into one immense, gray-blue, lightening sheet. I walked back to the rail, and after a while I turned to the boy. "Isn't it a little chilly to go barefoot, yet?"

He looked at me with a blank face that contracted into a frown. Then he shrugged.

Geo saw him too, now. He asked him, "Friend, was it raining at all last night? There's an awful lot of fog. It gives you a sort of funny feeling, when you can't tell where the water leaves off and the sky begins."

The boy made a gesture toward his mouth.

"You can't talk?" asked Geo.

The boy nodded.

Geo began to move his hands, and I realized he was talking sign language.

But the boy gave a bewildered look and turned his palms up.

"Where did you learn sign language?" I asked Geo. Then to the boy: "You don't understand?"

The boy nodded.

"Can you hear?"

Again the boy nodded. He had dark eyes that sank down into their sockets when you looked at him. "Oh," said Geo. "What's your name?"

The boy reached in his shirt and fingered out a chain with a metal dog tag on the end.

Geo took it from his hand and we looked at it. There was just the one word, "Snake."

"Snake?" said Geo. "That's your name?"

The boy nodded.

"My name's Geo," Geo said. "This is Jimmy."

The boy nodded through the gray night ending, and then smiled. We shook hands. Meanwhile Geo was digging in his pocket, and came up with the working half of a pencil and paper. "We've just had a night of it," Geo said. "Been from one end of the city to the other. What brings you down here?" He handed the boy the paper and pencil.

"Nowhere else to go," Snake wrote, a gawky printed hand that jerked the letters over the paper in the lucent grayness. He handed it back to us and grinned, apologizing probably for his evasiveness.

"Where do you live?" I asked.

He shrugged.

"I'm a writer," volunteered Geo, which is the only time I've ever before or since heard him introduce himself to anyone like that.

Snake looked interested, and then he pointed to the fogged and indistinct figures of the others around the deck.

"Yeah," said Geo. "Those are ours. We came with them."

Snake nodded, and then made a questioning look.

"Who are they?" said Geo. "Just people. Some of them are sort of funny people."

Snake nodded. Then he turned to the rail again, and pointed out to the undefined gray about us.

"Yeah, it is," said Geo.

My sister joined us now, her arms folded from the cold. "Brrrrr," she said. "Hello," she smiled at Snake.

"Margaret, this is Snake. Snake, this is my sister Margaret," I said, "Hello," Margaret said again, and she shook his hand.

Snake took the pencil and wrote something and gave it to me.

"You have a pretty sister," it said.

When I read it, he laughed.

"Thank you," Margaret said, smiling. "Geo?"

"What?"

"Who is Bill Sloan?"

"Huh? Oh, he's a man I know. A good friend of mine. Why do you ask?"

"Someone mentioned him to me in connection with you at the party, only I wasn't quite sure what the connection was."

"He sort of took me under his wing a couple of years ago and gave me a push in the right direction."

"Someone mentioned him to me too," I said. "Nobody was talking about anything but you at that place."

Geo shrugged.

"I was just wondering," Margaret said.

The four of us stood there now, leaning against the railing, gazing into the featureless sea. The dim sourceless light lined the edges of faces and bleached out features. "Do you live in Staten Island?" Geo asked.

Snake shook his head.

"In New York then."

Snake shook his head again.

"Where do you sleep?" Geo inquired.

Snake shrugged, and then pointed into the cabin of the ferry.

"Oh," said Geo, and laughed.

"Don't you talk sign language?" Margaret asked Geo. "I remember you could when you used to come over to our house years ago."

"I do," said Geo. "But Snake doesn't."

"Oh," she said, turning to Snake. "You can't talk, can you?"

Snake shook his head.

"How come you never learned?"

He grinned and shrugged.

"Why can't you talk?" she asked.

Snake opened his mouth and made a scissors with his fingers in front.

"No tongue?" asked Margaret. "You were born that way?"

Snake shook his head.

"It wasn't cut out?"

Snake nodded, and Margaret winced. "How long ago?"

The boy held up two fingers.

"When you were two years old?"

Snake shook his head again.

"Two months?"

Snake nodded.

"Oh, I'm sorry," Margaret said. "I suppose I shouldn't have asked."

He shrugged and smiled again.

Then he took the paper and wrote: "That's all right." We watched before the veil of the receding pearl. The breeze about us bit into necks and the corners of the eyes.

Geo said, "Look, if you've really got no place to sleep, you can come home with me. My wife won't mind and we've got a couch. You can stay for a couple of days until you get some place of your own. It's still a little cold at night to sleep on the ferry."

Snake shrugged and smiled a sort of three quarters consent. And then the silence and the fog and the weight of day burst in me like the release of falls, and I suddenly relaxed against the rail, aware how tired, voyager, I was; my eyes lost themselves ahead of me in the mist, deep, and deeper into the film pulling from the night and still on the day, water rippling into sky and nothingness before us over the side. We would have to come back across the river. We would have to go home. But the instant caught itself fixed in fog, in the sound of broken waves, and receding rhythm of gray water.

PART TWO

I. In Praise of Limestone

"... Not yet in full,
Yet in some arbitrated part
Order the façade of the listless summer."[167]
— James Agee

1.

I came into Margaret's room while she was sitting at her desk reading. The lamp made light like yellow jasper on the wood. "I'm going down to Geo's now," I said. "Did you finish with it yet?"

"I'm just about halfway through," she told me, sitting back. "You know, the Sloans must be a very strange family."

"Yeah, I guess so. Geo must be sort of strange too," I said. "I guess I can bring the manuscript some other time; I just

[167] This is from the introductory verses to James Agee's *Let Us Now Praise Famous Men*.

wanted to see if I could catch his wife, though. You want to come?"

"I'll finish this and come some other time," Margaret said. "Mother's been in here once; I think someone ought to stay home."

"Oh, O.K.," I said, and then left the room. I descended through the late August evening that filled our house now. Outside, walking down the street, the sky was turquoise between the buildings.

2.

I walked into Geo's apartment, and he said to me: "She's not here. She left."

"What do you mean?" I asked.

"She left," he said. "God damn it, she left."

"Wait a minute," I said. "Will you tell me exactly what happened?" Snake was sitting on the couch with his hands in his lap. He looked up at me when I came in. "My sister's still reading your play so I couldn't bring it down to you," I told Geo. "I guess you can have it tomorrow."

Geo began to scratch his head, and then suddenly said, "God damn," and whirled from the living room out toward the kitchen. I heard the bathroom door slam, and (questioningly) looked at Snake. He shrugged.

"What's been going on?" I asked.

He shrugged again.

"Did you meet his wife?" I asked, speaking quietly.

Snake nodded.

The flush box roared in the bathroom.

"What's she like? You mean she just left him like that?"

Geo came into the living room again. "Why do people have to go to the bathroom at such damn silly times," he demanded. "Do you want something to eat?"

"What's in the icebox?" I said. "I'll fix it. Hey, Snake, would you run out and get a dozen cans of beer?" I gave him more money and then went into the icebox. There was a lot of last night's dinner, and I put most of it in a pan with a pad of butter and a quarter of a cup of water. "This is to make up for not slicing the onions last night," I called to Geo.

I heard the couch give; he had slung himself on his stomach, when I looked, and was reading a book. Snake got back, dinner got eaten, and the three of us drank six cans of beer very quickly.

"You know," Geo said finally, looking at his empty can, "if I talked, this stuff would last longer, wouldn't it?"

"Yeah," I said.

"But I don't know what the hell to say."

"Well, what happened, after you and Snake got home?"

"She was here, then," Geo said. "I asked her where she'd been, just nicely, mind you. She said she'd been out. I explained about the mix up with the invitations. She said she knew I'd forgotten to mail them and she had just decided she didn't want to be here. She wasn't up to it, she said. I asked her if she minded Snake being here. No, she didn't. I went to bed. I went to sleep. Then, suddenly, she was waking me up. She looks at me real strangely, and then she says, *I'm leaving you.* Then she took her hand off my shoulder, and I saw she had her coat on. I thought she was going to the store. *When are you coming back?* I asked.

I'm not, she said, and she'd already started away.

I jumped up out of my bed in my damn underpants and said, *Hey, look, why?*

I'm not happy, she said. She was already opening the door. *I'm not happy. You're not happy.* And then she said, *Look, will you leave me alone?* And then she went out."

I glanced at Snake for corroboration, but he sat listening on the floor, his arms over his knees, holding his can of beer, dark eyes toward Geo.

"Where do you think she's gone?" I asked.

"How should I know," Geo said. "If I knew, I'd be there."

"People don't move from one situation to another unless two things are true. The one they're in must be unpleasant, and they can think of a pleasanter one to get to. I have no idea what Laile didn't like here, and I don't know what she thought would be better."

"Which means," said Geo, "you can't tell me why she left or where she went. It also implies that I can. I don't know, Little Brother, I wish I could, but it seems so damn hard."

"What exactly have you been doing recently?" I said. "What's been going on in your life?"

"That's a good question," Geo said.

"In fact what's been happening since you got your first book of poems published?"

"Well, there was the summer before that when I first met the Sloans, which is also where I met Frost. You left my notebook open, incidentally to the pages you were browsing in. I came back to the city, published. I got married, we went to Europe for ten months. We came back. Since then I've been doing little things in magazines. And just recently Bill Sloan has been urging me to get another book together."

"When did you go to Europe?" I asked. "And when did you write that play? And how recently have you spoken to Bill Sloan?"

"I went to Europe about a year ago. I wrote the play between the time I got married and the time I left for Europe. And the last time I heard from Mrs. Sloan was two weeks ago. And what are you so excited about?"

"Nothing," I said. "What about Mr. Sloan? We'll work backwards. When did you hear from him, what did he say, and what was your wife doing?"

"I told you, about two weeks ago. He sent me a letter; here, wait a minute, I'll get it." He jumped up and went into the dark room, and returned with a couple of folded sheets of paper. "I sent him some stuff, and he read them and sent back this. He thinks I should go about getting it published."

I took the sheets of paper and read:

August 15, 1962

THE MOST EXASPERATING THING IN THE WORLD IS UNDISCIPLINED GENIUS. Everyone hesitates to impose restraints — for fear of taming the whirlwind. Everyone balks at channeling the flowing stream — for fear of tampering with the spring. Everyone backs away from the raging flames for fear of denying them fuel.

Too often the whirlwind howls over the ultimate horizon, leaving only a patternless trail of destruction, without once precipitating a rain-cloud on the parched earth, without once lifting the galleon-sails, without once clearing the polluted air that veils the sun.

Too often the flood spends itself in harmless dispersion, without bringing sustenance to thirsty roots, without leaving a single pool where flashes of silver, blue-black and speckled green trouble the reflections, with no slightest trickle to mark the bubbling fount from which it came. And what is more desolate than a burned-out fire? Cold ashes with no memory of a gold and crimson, with no lingering truth, with no hint of what they were before consummation.

Geo:

There is no word for the intoxicating excitement that accompanies discovering you.

Equally, there is no adequate phrase for my anger at your determination to make a sow's ear out of a silk purse.

I will agree that every artist has to find his own discipline, that he should not be a conscious imitator, that he must, according to his bent, be an innovator.

BUT, HE MUST NOT FALL IN LOVE WITH HIS INNOVATION. HE MUST NOT SO SELF-CONSCIOUSLY RESIST IMITATION THAT HE STIFLES ORIGINALITY. HE MUST NOT DECEIVE HIMSELF WITH THE BELIEF THAT ANY CAPRICIOUS "ORDER" IS SELF-DISCIPLINE.

(Here the typewriter ribbon switched to red):

No — this does not all apply to you or, rather, all of it applies occasionally but none to the degree that might seem to be implied.

(Back to black typewriter ribbon:)

I know how many disagree with the statement that "The aim of artistic creation . . . (is) an ideal work in which (the real) is corrected . . . the ambition of the (artist) is to take the imperfect and unsatisfying reality and to transform it into a perfect, unified and satisfying whole." Nevertheless, I am prepared to defend it against all arguments.

There is no mirror that you can hold up to nature; "to show virtue her own feature, scorn her own image, and the very age and body of the time his form and pressure" — except the magic mirror of *your own invention* — which reflects only so much as you choose. There is no glass, nor can there be, that reflects all. (Nor one that reflects nothing.)

But why choose to hold the mirror up in the first place?

(That's not a fair question, and I withdraw it.)

You did choose. In "good faith" you have invented your mirror which, in almost every way, is so exciting in what it reflects that one grows impatient with unclear or badly distorted areas.

This is written right after reading THE FALL OF THE TOWERS and though you may damn me to a fare-the-well — my criticism remains the same.

OF COURSE YOU MUST BE SATISFIED — YOU THE CREATOR — but if you fail to communicate what you want to say or imply, can you be really satisfied?

Yes, it is beautifully done (as though you didn't already know that) but again you play fast and loose with *time.* If the meaningless of *time* is what you want, you've got to "cue" your reader "in" (as I said of other things).

Your fear of being too obvious is understandable. I don't think *you* could be. And let me illustrate the mechanics of the thing.

I cannot, and no more can you, imagine a poem of substance beginning:

> Arbitrarily I am going to assign
> Colors to the vowels
>   and then
> Compose a symphony of images

However, there is such a poem, that "cues in" the reader in the way that I mean:

> *A noir, E blanc, I rouge, U vert, O bleu: voyelles,*
> *Je dirai quelque jour vos naissances latentes:*
> *A, noir corset velu des mouches éclatantes*
> *Qui bombinent autour des puanteurs cruelles,*
>
> *Golfes d'ombre . . .*

And you know the rest of it, I know. It remains one of the most perfect sonnets in the French language even if our friend Rimbaud did *demonstrate* in the first line exactly what he was doing.

This remains my biggest criticism. Why not take some of the smaller pieces, for which I find no great faults, and go through "the horror of publication" and leave all THE FALL.

I write this, as usual, to think in visible form and also because I am not sure we will get a chance to discuss it when we next meet, if only because of myriad people who avail themselves of my hospitality during your visits.

Bill

P. S. IT'S GREAT. WHY NOT GREATER?

"He didn't invite you to visit him, recently, did he?" I asked.

"No," Geo said.

After that I couldn't think of too much. "Where has Laile been that she's liked recently?" I inquired, finally.

"Why?" Geo asked.

"She may have gone back. What about parents?"

"No," said Geo. "That, no."

"Has she enjoyed being anyplace?"

"Apparently not here."

"I gather that. But there must have been something pleasant during the past six months."

"Probably the most pleasant time was the time she was away from me," said Geo disgustedly.

"When was that."

"For a month, July, she had a job at a summer camp. I think she liked that, but she was only hired for a month."

"You mean summer camp taking care of children?"

Geo nodded.

"Don't those usually last till the end of August? Maybe she went back. There'd still be a week to go."

"What for?"

"Maybe there was someone she liked up there. Another counselor whom she made friends with."

"You're nuts," Geo said. He rolled to his feet. "Let's take a walk." He mussed Snake's hair. "Come on, kid." We got up, threw jackets on, and followed him into the hallway.

We dropped on the street and passed beneath the mercury flares above the alley that bleached the gray brick walls nearly purple and covered our faces, even Snake's, darker than mine, with silver pallid salve.

"Let's head over to the Village," Geo said.

"O. K.," I agreed, absently.

We passed the two block stretch of ruin, dead now, hills of cinder, featureless beyond the streetlamps.

"I wonder what happened to it?" I mused, "I don't think it could have burned out since last night."

Snake made an obscene gesture at his crotch.

"Huh?" said Geo. "Oh, the firemen I guess were here and watered it down."

"When did you see that?" I asked Snake.

He clapped his hands and pointed from himself to me.

"That means when he went to see you," Geo explained.

"I understood," I said.

Geo clapped his hands now. "That means 'when'."

"Are you teaching him sign language?" I asked.

"We're making it up as we need it."

Soon we reached the Village, and the pale leaves beneath the lights in the square shook over the benches in the dark. Coolness touched the night early, broke black through the advance of translucent darkness and made us hunch shoulders a little. "It must be cold as a bitch up in Massachusetts these nights."

I couldn't connect it to anything at first, but then I asked, "Is that where the camp Laile was working was at?"

"Uh-huh," Geo said.

We passed by a few people, turned down MacDougal Street, and sided the red brick front of the Provincetown Playhouse and on by yellow windowed coffee shops and white display cases in jewelry stores in which were scattered twists of silver, chains and jade.

A girl with a guitar case was coming toward us.

"Hi," said Geo. "Hello again."

"Hello," said Ann. "I was just on my way to the place you caught me coming from last night."

"Oh," Geo said. "That's right, you're singing there. How was your party? I went to one that was lousy."

"All right, I guess," said Ann. Her hair suddenly leapt across her shoulder with a breeze, and with her free hand she pushed it back. "That reminds me," she went on, "do you know anybody who's going up to Harvard in the next day or so?"

"No, why?"

"I've got a concert to do up there," she grinned. "Isn't that great?"

"How'd that happen?" asked Geo. "Yeah, I guess it is."

"At the party I was at. I met some guy who was arranging a hootenanny at Harvard. It's for Monday afternoon, sort of a going away thing for the summer session. He'd heard me before, and he wanted me to go up there. He said that if there was any way I could get a ride up there, I would be in it."

"You get paid?" asked Geo.

"Yep," said Ann. "If I can get there."

"Incidentally," said Geo, "this is my friend, Snake, and this is Jimmy."

"I think I met you before," Ann said to me.

"Last night," I said.

"Hello," she said to Snake. He nodded to her.

"As a matter of fact we might be going up in that direction tomorrow afternoon."

"Oh, you're kidding," said Ann.

"No, I'm serious," said Geo. "Do you know where I live?"

"Somewhere over east," Ann said. "I don't know where though."

"On Fifth Street," said Geo. He gave her the house number. "Get there about four-thirty, and we'll give you a ride up."

"If you're not kidding me," said Ann, "I'll be there."

"I'm not kidding."

"All right. I don't think I'll find anybody else going up there at this time of year, before tomorrow, anyway." She hefted up the bulky guitar case now. "Look, I've got to get going. I'm probably late already. I'll see you tomorrow, then." And she was off, lugging the instrument case down toward the awning of a bright-lit coffee shop.

"Why and how are you going up to Harvard?" I asked Geo. "And what the hell is this 'we' business?"

"Don't you want to go up to the hootenanny at Harvard?" Geo asked, innocently. Then, matter of factly, "Look, Harvard is in Cambridge, Cambridge is in Massachusetts, and so is Laile's camp."

"I thought you said it was a silly idea about her going back there."

"It is," said Geo. "Can you think of a better one?"

"I don't know?" I said.

"Well, I can't. And if you do, tell me."

"All right," I said. "Fine. I know why. Now tell me how."

"I have resources," said Geo. "Among them a driver's license."

"Can you get a car?"

"I can get a car."

"Oh," I said.

"Do you two want to come along?"

I took a breath. "All right," I said. "I'll come."

Snake nodded.

"Great," said Geo. We started walking again. "Incidentally," said Geo, "I'll be busy in the morning. Can you do something for me?"

"What is it?"

"I've got some manuscripts at my parents' house that I want to get down here. Could you run over and pick them up?"

"Tomorrow? Sure."

"They're in an envelope in my room on my work table. I don't think you'll have any trouble getting them. Did you ever meet my parents?"

"You mother, once," I said. "Years ago."

"Oh, that's right. Well, if you can get the manuscripts and bring them down with you when you come, you'll save me some trouble."

"Sure," I said. "What time do you want me?"

"Well, you can either come around twelve with me to get the car, or around four-thirty with Ann. It doesn't matter."

"Twelve," I said.

"All right," answered Geo. "Hey!" Because Snake suddenly turned away from us and began to run down the street. "What the hell?" said Geo. And then, "Come on!"

We ran after him. He was dodging people, and, I finally realized, following something. Because suddenly he cut across the street. Geo and I angled after him.

"Watch out!" I suddenly yelled. And Geo's hand slapped down on a sudden car fender and he leapt back four feet. The car lunged forward on its springs and rocked back to a standstill. The driver was starting to get out and say something, because I saw the door opening, but Geo skirted around in front of it; I came around behind, and we joined on the opposite corner of the street.

"Where the hell did he go?" Geo asked, panting.

I looked down the block. "I don't see him."

"He couldn't have gotten all the way down the block between now and then," said Geo. We looked around.

"Maybe he ducked into one of the doorways." We started down the block again, checked, but didn't find him. Halfway up the other side, Geo said, "You know, this is silly. We're not going to find him in here. Besides, I don't think he's hiding from us."

"It looked like he saw something go by and decided to follow it."

"Whatever it was, it must have been going pretty damn fast."

"Maybe it was a car," I suggested. "I wonder if he's gone for food?"

"I hope not," said Geo. "I hope he doesn't get himself hurt."

"Hurt?" I asked.

"What sort of a person goes and gets his tongue cut out?" Geo asked. "I don't think it would be too gross a statement to say someone like that was—accident prone?"

"I sort of assumed it was for something medical," I said.

"Yeah, so did I," said Geo. "I asked him about it last night. No. Some vicious cat went and cut his tongue out."

"Why?" I asked.

"He wouldn't say," Geo said.

We started walking again. The streets we had come to now were as silent as the streets of the Village had been noisy. The quiet was dust suspended in the air, or, somehow, like a silver ball-bearing hovering in the hollow ear.

"I remember once," Geo started, "a friend of mine had read something I wrote, and then looked at me very earnestly and said, 'There's a lyric quality in your work which I find unique with . . . G. K. Chesterton!'" He laughed. "I guess that was supposed to be a compliment. I'd never read G. K. Chesterton, and I still haven't. But, nothing against him, it seems like a funny way to compliment somebody."

"Why?" I asked. "And what brings that up?"

"As a matter of fact I was thinking about my mother," said Geo. "And you going up to pick up those manuscripts. That's the sort of compliment she is very fond of giving me."

"What sort of person was your father?" I asked.

"A good question." He shrugged. "I don't really know. What sort of person was yours?"

"I guess I asked you so I could help figure it out for me."

"I figured," said Geo. "Only I still can't give you any answer."

We walked through the silence of stone walls, a quietness defined by the broken blocks of east-side paving stones and the receding lucence of the red night sky. Quiet filled the crevices of the streets, as the tar filled cracks in the cement blocks of Broadway, which we crossed now, lavid fissures of black on mottled gray. Here they had not yet installed mercury vapor lamps; instead of white, Geo's face was washed with a soft yellowish glow, at least yellowish after the magnesium hardness of the Square's light. And then there were two blocks with no illumination at all, and we had only our footsteps with us, and the paleness of night beyond high house tops. At last we turned down the alley, lit white and hard now, toward Geo's building.

And then into the black hallway.

We climbed the stairs, came toward the apartment door, when we both nearly stumbled over something at the same time. Whatever it was sprang open like a trap, and then Geo knocked his door open, and the light which fell out now left the three of us blinking at each other.

"Snake, what the hell is the matter with you?" said Geo. "Oh, come on inside. Where in the world did you get to."

We walked into the kitchen. Snake looked from one of us to the other.

"Were you sleeping in front of the door?" Geo asked.

Snake nodded.

"Hey," I said. There was a long gash on the mute boy's dark forearm. And there was a rough, clotted scab on the side of his jaw about the size of a half dollar.

Geo saw too.

"There is alcohol in the bathroom, and cotton, and gauze," he said. "Get yourself cleaned up."

Snake went off into the bathroom. Geo and I looked at each other and I shrugged. "What do you think happened?" I mouthed. This time Geo shrugged.

We went into the living room, and after a while he came in swabbing the gash on his arm with a swab of cotton. The black down on his arm lay flat on either side of the cut beneath the moving cotton. He'd put a bandage on his jaw, but one end of the arm's wound still welled blood.

He looked at us from the doorway, silently, and from beneath his eyebrows' dark ridge.

"You want some help with that?" I asked.

We got the adhesive tape and the gauze and the Merthiolate and lined his dark arm with a strip of white.

Geo brought over the pad and paper. "Can you tell us what happened?" he asked, offering the writing material to Snake.

Snake looked at the paper, then at Geo. Then he shook his head.

"I should have figured as much," said Geo. "I'm going to quell my curiosity and not ask again," he announced. "But if you ever can tell me, I wish you would."

3.

When I got home, my eyes were filled with the bright liquid of fatigue. Walking up the stairs, the walls seemed far away, and movement quickly became unfelt and mechanical.

The light fell through the doorway of the living room. I looked in.

"Jimmy?"

"Yes, Mom?" I said.

"Where have you been?"

She was sitting in the arm chair in a dark green bathrobe that came tight around her neck.

"Just out to a friend's house," I said. "You know Geo Keller."

She looked at me with her hands on the edge of her chair. The white stalks of her fingers grew into arcs on the leather arms. "Don't you have any respect for your dead father?" she asked, in a voice that was hoarsely flowering in the back of her throat.

"What do you mean, Mom?" I asked.

"You know what I mean. You cannot go out and stay up so late, running around the city. It is disrespectful to the memory of . . ."

I turned from the room; I didn't mean to fling the door closed, at least I don't think I did. But it exploded too, and my mother's voice screamed "Jimmy!" on top of it.

I went to my room; once in inside, I found all the tiredness had condensed to one quivering diamond in the front of my skull which would not relax into sleep.

At last, still dressed, I came outside into the hall. Either the sound of my opening door, or simply simultaneity of impulse had made my mother decide to come from the living room; we turned into the hall at the same time, stopped, and stared.

I think she was going to speak, but all she ended by doing was raising her head. The axis of fear that seemed to pinion her from neck to knee was revolving slowly before me. My shoulders were shaking, I realized.

"Jimmy," she said, lowering her head again, down so her chin was on her chest. "You can't leave again. You can't . . ."

"Mom," I said, "I'm going with Geo up to Harvard tomorrow to take a friend of his. . . . Mom, we'll only be gone . . ."

But she had raised her hands above her head, and suddenly she ran forward. The bathrobe, only closed at the neck, blew wide and flapped against both walls of the hallway as she came. I whirled back into my room, grabbed the doorjamb and averted my face against it as she came.

Then she had passed me. I looked up slowly. The door to her room was open; I started to approach it. She was crying inside.

I wanted to say something. Just "Mother." But the mask of my face had locked so tightly I couldn't open my mouth. I backed down the hall to my room, turned off the light, and lay down on my bed until morning.

4.

The next day I told Margaret about the coming trip with Geo. "So I get stuck with her again," she said, looking at me.

"Would you rather I didn't go?"

"Don't be silly. I would if I had the chance." Then she smiled. "But thanks for asking."

"You want to come along and pick up Geo's manuscripts with me?"

"Where?"

"At his house. Have you ever been there?"

"No. Sure I'll come." We went down the stairs and out into the street. Margaret scrunched up her face and sniffed deeply. "Wow, does this smell good. You've got a fine day for a car ride." Then she asked, "Which way does Geo live?"

When we got to the old block where Geo's mother's house was, I pointed out the red brick building to Margaret.

"It's the smallest house on the block," she said.

"I remember it as being large and Gothic," I told her.

Once we reached the dark vestibule she looked around and said, "Well, it's certainly Gothic enough."

There were tiny tufts of carpeting on tacks around the floor. Before us an ornate bannister edged a narrow stairway to the second floor. Just above my head hung a black iron chandelier. What had once been candle holders were now wired for electric light sockets and the new wiring that wound each arm made it look as though it had been caught in webs.

A woman in a dark dress appeared at the stair's head.

"What do you want," she barked down through the darkness.

"Mrs. Keller?"

"Yes."

"I'm a friend of your son, Geo. He asked me to pick up some manuscripts for him. He says they're in an envelope on his work table."

"Who are you?"

"My name is Jimmy Calvin," I called back. "This is my sister Margaret."

She descended the stairs smoothly and slowly, like something mechanical. Her dress, I saw came down below her ankles. She was almost exactly my height. Her hair, thin, hugged her skull tightly, and was completely white.

When she reached the bottom, she regarded me for a moment and then said, "I've never met you, have I."

"Once," I said. "But that was years ago. Geo and I went to school together."

"Were you one of the friends he used to bring home?"

"I only met you once," I said.

"My son sent you for some of his writing?"

"Yes, ma'am," I said.

"Will you come upstairs with me?"

She turned and we followed her up to the second floor. There were all sorts of rooms opening from the hall. She took a set of keys from her pocket and opened one door. "This is my son's room," she said.

Inside were two beds, bookshelves, and a work table on which were mostly bundles of paper. She went to the table, pocked up an envelope and came back to us. "This must be the one he means." She paused before we left. "I keep his room clean for him," she said. "I keep it spotless." Then she closed the door behind us, and once more locked it. "How is my son?" she asked. "Won't you have a cup of coffee before you go. I hear very little from him."

"Yes, thank you," I said.

"Come with me. I had already begun to make some for myself, so it will be no bother."

She led us into a large bedroom. There were gilt framed portraits on the wall and the high posts of the bed were knobbed with ivory carvings.

Chairs sat around a coffee table that squatted on carved paws. A white china coffee pot trailed a cream colored cord to the floor, the only thing to show it was electric. We sat around the table, and Mrs. Keller poured coffee into white cups. Then we were offered silently the sugar and the cream.

"How is he?" she asked again. "I see him seldom. And his girl, how is she."

"They're fine," I said.

"Did he send his love to me?"

After a silence, my sister volunteered, "Yes. He wants to know how you are, and he said he hoped you were well."

"Good," said Mrs. Keller. Without relaxing at all, she leaned back in her chair. "Very good." She stared at the black circlet of liquid in the porcelain she held in her hands. "It is hard," she said. "He is a very difficult person. Like his father in many ways. But his father is very sick."

"Mr. Keller isn't well?" asked Margaret.

"Mr. Keller has not been well for years. He had to be put away." She spoke with a gray harshness in her voice. "Not at all well," she repeated. She looked up, now. "He is in a sanitarium near Chicago. That is near his home. The boy and his father do not get along well. The distance, you see, ends an excuse for visits which both would wish and both would resent if it were at all possible. You see?" she repeated. "You see?"

Margaret nodded.

Suddenly she sat straight again. "My love for my son is perfect. You must tell him that he may come back whenever he wishes. You must tell him. . . . I would like to see him." She paused. Then smiled. "No, you must not tell him that." She put her cup upon the table, and light leaped into the dark liquid.

"You may go."

We rose, took the envelope, and preceded Mrs. Keller into the hall. As she closed the door behind her she said, "I have enjoyed seeing you."

We said good-bye and walked downstairs, and out beneath the arthropod chandelier. The day was still vivid.

"Will you write?" Margaret asked. "You didn't before."

"I'm not going to be gone that long. Just a couple of days."

"Oh," said Margaret.

We walked slowly home.

"Underwear," Margaret said. "And socks. Sweater. I'm going to be a real expert in packing men's clothes. I hope I get a nice stay-at-home husband." She laughed. Then she said, "Jimmy I heard most of what happened last night."

"You did?"

"Um-hm." We wandered down the edge of the sidewalk, near the street, in the sun. "I don't understand it. She's not that way toward me. At least not so much. But she worries about you so much it's sick. So much that if I were you, I'd get the hell out and I wouldn't come back."

"I don't want to run away from anything," I said.

"I know, Jimmy. I'm not telling you to not come back. I don't know what the hell I'm telling you. Well, that I think you're probably very mixed up about a lot of things, that, I must admit, I'm sort of mixed up about too. With the result that I can't be too helpful."

"Sometimes I wish somebody would either be helpful or just shut up about them."

"Don't get mad, Jimmy."

"I'm not mad," I said. "But Geo was the last person who said that to me."

"Maybe he could help more than I could. He's older, for one thing."

"Help isn't what I'm looking for," I said.

"What are you looking for?"

"I don't know," I said. "Maybe some peace and quiet."

She smiled. "Well, you have a nice trip. I hope you have a good time."

"Thanks," I said. "I hope it isn't too tough on you while I'm gone."

"Don't be silly. Here, let's come on and get you packed."

We went upstairs, somehow avoided by my mother, and ended up with a limited and sensible assortment of clothes, toothbrush, and the whole thing wrapped in an army blanket and tied with brown twine.

At the door she handed me Geo's envelope. "Oh, and here's your coat. I know you can't wear it today, but it gets cold at night. I hope the hootenanny's fun, and I hope you find Laile. Say 'boo' to Geo for me, and, oh yes, I put his play in there with the other things. You've got a great day for driving."

"You want to come too?" I said.

She paused. "So much I can taste it. Now go on." She closed the door between us, and I was standing out in the street alone.

5.

I threw the blanket bundle on the bed. Geo came out of the bathroom and said, “Well, I was wondering when you’d get here. Manuscripts?”

“Right there.” I gave him the envelope. “Where’s Snake?”

He took it and peered inside. “Somewhere, I guess.”

The door opened, and Geo turned around. “Oh, here he is.” He closed the envelope. “I guess we can check these on the subway. Come on.”

“Where are we going?”

“To get a car.”

“Where do we get the car from?” By this time we were already out the door and halfway into the street. But Geo had opened the envelope again and was ruffling through the pages.

“What have you been doing?” I asked Snake.

He held one hand up and marched two fingers across his palm.

“Walking?”

He made a shape with his fingers.

“Over in the square?”

He nodded.

“Have you any idea where we’re going to get this car from?”

Snake shrugged.

We ambled through the cluttered slums of the Lower East Side, across trickling black gutters and through the beginning swell of heat that bloated garbage in the cans and burst the frosted skins of plums in the vendors’ stalls beneath awnings of rotting green canvas. Heavy flies exploded among grape clusters, syrup-sopped and sluggish.

We walked into the yellow-tiled subway entrance, and down beneath the low, barred ceiling. We jingled brass disks into the stile which clunked us through, and then the silence of the platform was hammered out by the blunt juggernaut's nose. We got on the train.

Geo immediately began to read through the sheaf of poems. Snake put his bare feet on the plastic-straw seat in front of him, and leaned back. Once a tall conductor came through, started to say something, and then walked on.

"Hey, here we are," Geo said, suddenly jumping up. Hardly aware that the train had stopped, I followed him, along with Snake. Upon the street, after passing through the grim clotted gateway of the above ground kiosk, I recognized our location, Broadway, perhaps a half mile below Columbia Circle.

Here the wide street leans toward the river, and through an open block, instead of the usual progression of houses, there was nothing, as if the city had been sheered brightly away.

We turned toward West End Avenue, passed on wide warm streets, and came finally to a gray awning that stuck like a beak over the sidewalk. The doorman slipped open a French glass door for us into an orange-lit lobby, cooler than the sidewalk. The room, breeze-filled and warm-hued, delved deeply into the building.

"Hi John," Geo said to the doorman, and to us, "This way."

We passed mirrors, and ended up before an elevator door. Once in the rising chamber, I asked, "Do you mind telling me who we're going to see?"

"Bill Sloan," Geo said.

"I should have known."

Snake was looking around the bronze band that rimmed the upper wall when the door opened. We followed Geo to the left; he rang three times at a dark mahogany door in the dull yellow wall.

Footsteps, the door opened. "Oh, Hi. Come in. Are these your friends?"

"Bill, this is Snake, and Jimmy."

Mr. Sloan looked down at Snake's feet. "Aren't you afraid of broken glass?"

Snake shook his head.

"Well, then, Hello."

We shook hands. Meanwhile Geo bounded off toward another room.

"Where did he go?" I asked.

Mr. Sloan shrugged.

He was a slightly balding, gray haired man. He was wearing a tee-shirt, slippers, and didn't look as if he were expecting company. "Well, come in. I'm not going to be made a party to his impoliteness." We were standing in a large foyer, nearly a quarter of which was taken up by a huge renaissance table, dark wood with gabled edges and columned legs. Beneath piled papers, phone books and a great lamp, I could see chipped ivory inlay patterned onto the wood. A hall pierced the right wall; two entrances fronted us. The larger was an arch leading into a white-ceilinged living room. Piano, a wide, wood rimmed sofa, oval-backed chairs, nests of chairs and book stands sat around the walls beneath several big paintings and a few smaller ones.

"Sit down; tell me about yourselves." As we sat, he did also, tucking one leg beneath him on a large chair.

I didn't say anything, and relaxed when Geo charged back into the room, still reading a sheaf of papers held in one hand, and handed Mr. Sloan a glass of iced coffee with the other. "I've already made it," he said, coming across the living room, "so don't ask me for it." He paused in the darker archway, and looked up. "You got your car keys?"

"I have the car keys," said Mr. Sloan.

Geo grinned back at him. "Thanks," he said, and disappeared beyond the arch.

"I assume you have the poetry," Mr. Sloan called after him.

"Yeah, right here," came Geo's voice diminishing down the hall.

"Fair trade," called Mr. Sloan again. "You know where to leave it." He turned back to us. "Jimmy," he said, musing. "Geo's mentioned you. You went to school together?"

"That's right," I said.

"What do you do now?"

"Right now I'm wasting my summer vacation," I said.

"And you?" he asked Snake.

Snake smiled and touched his mouth with his fingertips.

"He can't talk," I explained.

"Oh," said Mr. Sloan. "Oh, I see."

There was the silence of recovery that comes when the prepared direction of a conversation is suddenly blocked.

"Are you going up to Harvard for the concert?"

"More or less. Just for the trip, mainly."

"Oh, I see."

"What do you think of these new poems of Geo's?" I asked, wanting to get away from a subject that was leading to trivial silence.

"Have you read them?"

"Only a few," I said. "I'd looked at some of them on the train."

"I think they're very fine, in part." Suddenly he drew the smile from his face with a lifting of muscle along his cheeks. "I think they belong to a tradition that is very rare in American literature, a tradition which has been impossible to develop until now because there has been no 'scape on which to base it. It involves a discipline, you see, that was possible for such men like Coleridge, Shelley, and Byron to have, but not for Crane, Pound, even Eliot to reach first hand. It has nothing to do with classical languages, but with . . ." Here he stopped. "Perhaps I am overstepping myself. It occurs to me that I'm making a set speech that I've made half a dozen times to three times that many people. I should have more respect for his work than that."

"What do you mean?" I asked. "Go on."

"Well, I've said most of it. The only thing left of the speech is an addendum to critics, when you judge his work, judge it as something valuable outside itself, and with compassion for the inception of something unique and very important."

"I think you're an ass, Bill," Geo said, coming back into the room. "Who the hell did you say that to?"

"Did you find the keys?" said Mr. Sloan.

"Right here," said Geo. "Look, I don't want anybody to be kind to anything I do. I don't think anybody should."

"When are you kids going to get my car back to me?"

"Three or four days."

"Fine. I have the other one, but I just want to keep track of it."

"You'll get it back. Hey, look, as a favor to a friend, don't go around telling people to be kind, huh?"

"As a favor," Mr. Sloan said. "A deal."

"Thanks," Geo said. "I left the manuscripts in your office. Say hello to Julia when she gets in; let's go."

Snake and I rose and started toward the door. "Good-bye," I said.

"I'm glad to have met you," Mr. Sloan said rising. "I hope I meet you again."

"Oh," said Geo. "That play of mine is in there too. Could we stick that in and publish it too?"

"We most certainly could not," Mr. Sloan said.

"Oh," said Geo. "Well, I'll see you in about a week."

"Fine," said Mr. Sloan. He had walked us to the door. "Next time, bring your wife along. Julia and I don't seem to see much of her. We'll even give you dinner."

"Sure," said Geo. "Good-bye."

In the hall, the first, somewhat idiotic questions bounced out, "He trusts you with his car?"

"He should. He taught me how to drive."

And the second: "Didn't you tell him Laile had left."

"No," said Geo.

"Oh," I said. We went down in the elevator. Through the glass slab, we stopped. "How much chance do you think there is of finding her?" I asked.

"What's wrong with the sky," Geo asked, not answering, looking above the buildings across the street. There was a steady breeze blowing.

Snake made a trickling motion with his fingers.

"Snake says it's going to rain. Now what do you mean what's wrong with the sky?"

There was a darkening lucence above us, as though the clouds had been smeared with apricot powder. The air was damp, heavy in the palms and on the shoulders.

"How much chance . . ." I started again.

"Come on," Geo interrupted. "We better hurry."

We crossed the street and went down the inclined block toward Broadway. Again we crossed the large street and on one of the side streets, entered the wide door of a garage. Fluorescent tubes lined the ceiling and white razors cut the flanks of red and black metal or into the curves of windshields, bright as acetylene after the darkness in the street. "By the time we get home it will be raining," Geo commented, hurrying among the cars.

We found it, a dull green and a trifle squat among the larger, newer ones. We got in, keys clocked into the starter's whine, released into the thrum of the motor, and we moved out into the darker street.

We sped the blown wire of the highway, the river beside us, through the net of freighter booms and the squat funnels of passenger ships. On the other side of the highway, the city hung under mist, or white light.

When we turned off, the shadows of the underpass lapped over us like wings and our car ran stuttering along the cobbled dockside. Then we broke the dark city. Take a piece of blue paper and hold it in front of one eye, and look out at the street with the other. This was the electric and affixitive timber the air took, breaking before our windshield.

Geo and I were by either door, Snake sitting between us, bare flat feet on the felt floored hump. The air became bluer and rushed at the aslant triangular window opened to the side. We finally stopped at the smashed curbstone of Geo's block and climbed from the sprung seats onto the blowy sidewalk. Snake's over-long hair whipped forward as he climbed down and he brushed it back. "It's so dark," said Geo, frowning to the breeze as he locked the door.

"I thought it would be pouring cats and dogs by now," I said.

Upstairs at the apartment, Geo gave out the last of the previous night's beer. Snake sat on the floor, arms, locked by a hand on a wrist, around his knees in front of him. The white scar of bandage below his rolled sleeve lined his arm brightly. Occasionally he touched the patch on his jaw, before taking another slushy mouth of beer. The empty cave of his jaw resonated, so you could hear him drink over the stumped flesh's root.

"Sometimes I think she'll walk in the door, just like that," Geo said, from the couch.

"Really?" I asked.

"No, not really."

"How much of a chance do you think we'll have of finding her there?"

"I haven't answered that question twice today," Geo said, turning his beer can in his fingers. "And I'm not going to answer it a third time."

"I wasn't sure you heard," I said.

"I heard," he answered. "But why say one thing or the other and fool myself? I'm getting sort of tired of that." He looked up, now, "Say, you didn't have any parental trouble in order to go with me, did you?"

"None that I couldn't take care of," I said.

"Which means you did have trouble. Well," he sounded as though he were going on. But didn't.

"Suppose she does come back?" I finally asked. "To get things, maybe. Do you want to leave a note?"

"I suppose I should," Geo said. "You know it's funny. The ways we fool ourselves. We take a group of incidents: if they happen to somebody else, we smile, and say, 'Well, it's his own fault, and I bet that within the year thus and so will have happened.' And we're usually right. But the same incidents happen to us and we become so intent on details here and there that we can't establish the simplest pattern; and if anyone tried to point out the pattern we're falling into, woe be it to him."

"What are you talking about?"

"I'm talking about the fact that until a week — no, till the day before yesterday, had anyone bothered to ask me about my love for Laile, I would have said it was perfect. And yet, thinking back, I realize I've said things even to you which probably let you know it wasn't. So many things have happened that had they happened to someone else I would have said, the love there is dangerous and slipping. But I thought it was perfect. I wanted it to be."

"Maybe it was," I said.

"She left me, didn't she?" The voice sharpened to cynicism. "Maybe hers for you was imperfect."

"Don't be an ass," he said. "I mean, she was right; we weren't happy. I just feel like a fool for not connecting, and still not being able to connect, the unhappiness with things that happened between us."

"What did happen between you?" I asked. "You still haven't told me anything about her, or about you and her."

He laughed. "Someday, if I'm feeling particularly drunk, I may."

"As you said to Snake," I replied: "I'm not going to ask again."

"Thanks," he said. "For nothing."

We finished the beer. We talked about Harvard. "What's the name of the camp we're going to?" I asked.

"Camp Hillrod[168]," Geo told me.

"Have you ever been there before?"

"Once I went up to see her. Just for the day. I know how to get there." And then, later, he said, "Gee, it's getting dark outside."

"It still hasn't rained," I said.

"It must be getting on toward four o'clock." He turned to Snake. "You've never heard Ann sing, have you? Jimmy, I know you did."

"Yes," I said.

"She's very good." He stood up from the couch. "Hey, let's go downstairs and look at the sky."

---

[168] This summer camp was going to be modeled on Camp Woodland, which Delany had attended between 1951 and 1956, where he first met Pete Seeger and was exposed to a number of idealistic counselors, including Mary Davis (Stormé DeLaverie), who went on to produce *The Jewel Box Review* and gained fame in the Stonewall Riots of June, 1969.

"Might as well bring the junk along," I said. "If it's still not raining we can put it in the car before it starts." I picked my blanket roll up.

"You don't have any extra underwear?" Geo asked.

"Why?" I asked. "I've got some."

"My stuff is too big for Snake. He's more your size."

"I'll share what I've got," I said.

Geo hoisted a knapsack up over one shoulder and started for the door, "Gee," I said. "The last time I packed that many clothes, I stayed away nearly two months."

"Who knows," laughed Geo.

On the sidewalk it was like entering swift evening. We sluiced through the wind to the car, flung bundles into the back seat, and started to the stoop again. Once the wind stopped, and silence broiled loud enough to still us, and we turned to each other, questioning, but then the street swelled with moving air again and the skitter of paper on pavement, and woooosh against the trumpet of the ear.

Ann came round the far corner before us, her black hair flung back on the wind, once a turning fan at the side of her face, then filamental and dispersed, then flung again.

The heavy guitar case, an overnight bag, these and the wind swayed her walking, and after seeing us, she ducked her head forward and came on. Meeting at the stoop, case and bag veered forward into Geo's hand; he took them up calling, "Come on. The car's this way."

"Well, she said loudly over wind. "You weren't kidding," laughed, and caught at her hair. "Isn't this a funny wind?"

Yeah," said Geo. Without breaking stride he handed me Ann's bag.

"What have you got in here?" I asked at the sudden lug against my arm.

"I carried it all the way over from the Village," she said, losing a tan sweater that blew open and threatened to pull from her shoulders. "Are we going to have a hurricane?"

"Could be," said Geo.

He opened the trunk, wrested the bag from me, dumped it in; I handed him the others from the back seat, and these also went into the trunk; the back closed down tight, and suddenly I said, "Hey. Where's Snake."

Geo stood up from the trunk lock. "God damn," he said.

"He was with you a second ago," Ann said.

Up and down the block, only blown crud and crouched car hulks.

"Let's go," Geo said disgustedly. "Come one, pile in."

Ann and guitar case got in the back seat, Geo and I in the front. Doors slammed on the broiling air and we rolled forward.

We did not speak.

Mist whipped on the building faces, and without currents the dampness could be felt. Peered at through darkening windows, the buildings seemed to run together, no; rather their surfaces were translucence behind which deep purple liquid flushed. Gray lengths of windows were regular tracks streamed on brown and red broken faces, all in false twilight.

"Look at the fog," Ann suddenly said, and down a passing street, three quarters across the city, a welling of blue fog had gathered in layers under an orange tinting in the sky.

Geo was driving very slowly, looking out his side window frequently.

"What are you looking for?" I asked.

"Three guesses," he said.

"Hey, there he is," I bawled. We'd gone maybe two blocks. The car stopped and my feet slammed on still moving ground as I ran toward Snake who was walking up the sidewalk. Geo's was right after me.

He turned, saw us, and sprinted forward, only to duck into a store ten feet ahead. I crashed in behind him, and stopped.

It was a tiny room with whitewashed walls and great cages on the side. The wind was replaced with the miniature thunders of — suddenly fives birds tumbled from a shelf high on the wall. Swirled the air in spirals around Snake, who had turned toward me, bare feet wide on the saw-dusted floor — pigeons.

A couple of boys and an older man were working in a further room; a kitten the color of cream, powdered with nutmeg and turmeric walked across the floor, rubbed Snake's ankle, and sprawled half on his bare foot.

"Hey," I said. "Come on."

He waited. His hand closed into fists, then opened again. He was breathing slowly and deeply.

Geo's voice was behind me: "Don't you want to come?"

Silence.

One of the boys walked from the back room with "Can I help you?" on his lips but stopped at the door.

"We really meant it," Geo said. "You can come. No problem. No questions."

Snake looked from one of us to the other.

A bird, white and nearly in slow motion, suddenly sailed toward him and swept against his chest. His hands flew up surprised, and then he was cuddling the bird against his stomach, holding gently white feathers.

He came forward now, with the bird.

The kid at the door said, “Hey, what do you people want?”

I looked around at the cages. “Nothing,” I said. “What is this place?”

Prideful balls of feathers strutted the floors at the pens. Lines of white birds perched chest high beside me.

“Pigeon store,” the boy said. “Do you want something?”

“No,” said Geo. “We’re just looking.”

Snake came to us, now, and suddenly white feathers exploded in his hand and the bird was gone.

“Hey, close the door,” the kid said. “I don’t want them to get out.”

We turned, and I saw Ann had come too. She seemed completely bewildered, but quiet.

“You sure it’s all right?” Geo asked Snake.

He looked up at Geo, without a movement.

Geo smiled. “Come on,” he said.

We all went back to the car, through the ululant wind.

“What do they sell pigeons for?” I asked Geo, once we had started again.

“Haven’t you seen pigeon flocks on the roofs down here?”

“You must have seen them flying,” Ann said from the back seat.

“Oh,” I said. “That’s what they’re for?”

“Um-huh,” said Geo.

Snake sat quietly in the back with Ann. As we hit the highway beneath the spires of the bridge, contorted wings like dragons, like dulled silver, the rain broke blue splendor on the windshield, washing away the city and the road.

"What are you thinking about?" Geo asked me.

"My father, as a matter of fact," I answered. "I'm trying to remember him."

"Between life and death," Geo said, "there's a bridge called dying. It's uncomfortable to watch people cross it."

"Yeah," I said.

Later, under the hushed rain, Ann took her guitar out in the backseat and tuned it. The notes were clear in the motor's whirr.

Once tuned, her fingers thrummed the strings in a chord that dropped a complete whole tone, wound in on itself with a webbing of fingers, and then raised again. On this background, repeated again and again, her voice touched the opening note with the clarity of snapped glass.

> "I was born in Portland town,"

she began to sing, the tuning anchored to the oscillating accompaniment.

> "I was born in Portland town,
> Yes I was, yes I was,"

the voice descending into a surprising chest register,

> "Yes I was,"

until a final note sunk low into the webbed sound of plucked strings.

> "I was married in Portland town,
> I was married in Portland town,"

and I turned around to look now.

"Yes, I was, yes I was, yes I was."

She sat sideways against the side of the car, her feet curled under her, looking down at her fingers on the instrument. Snake, beside her, watched with a half-open mouth. His lips were moving slowly, almost with hers.

"I had children, one two three,
I had children, one two three,"

she looked up now her length of black hair slipped down her shoulder and swung back over her sweatered arm.

"Yes I did, yes I did, yes I did."

"Well, they sent my children off to war,
Sent my children off to war."

Snake suddenly raised his hand, halted, and then reached forward.

"Yes they did, yes they did, yes they did."

He leaned forward, and the dark fingers fell on the side of her throat, and then slipped around.

"I don't have no kids no more,
I don't . . ." she paused, kept up the rhythm, and caught the words again,

". . . have no kids no more,
No I don't . . ."

His lips were moving with hers.

" . . . No
I don't . . ."

She stopped now and then her fingers stopped.

Snake took his hand away, his face gone into hurt puzzlement.

"I'm sorry," she said. "I'm . . . sorry."

Snake put his hands together into a cup and extended them toward her. She looked puzzled.

Geo, who had been watching in the rear view mirror said, "He's asking your pardon. I think he wants you to go on."

"You didn't do anything," Ann explained, hurriedly. "I didn't mean to stop."

She took a breath and began to play again. She raised her head, and then she began once more, bright above the car motor:

"I was born in Portland town,
I was born in Portland town.
Yes I was, yes I was, yes I was."